His head came closer, his lips brushing hers before he whispered, "Vicki, love." Then he was kissing her, deeply, lovingly.

Rising onto her toes, she pushed against his chest, kissed him back, her tongue darting into his mouth to taste. She had missed this, him, so much it hurt. Her blood heated as she continued to return his kisses. "Cole," she murmured against his mouth as his hands spread across her waist.

He lifted her, sat her on top of the washing machine, pushed his hips between her legs and continued kissing, continued ramping up her desire, turning her body into an inferno of need. This was them. This was how they'd got back together every time he'd been away.

This was bad timing. They hadn't resolved a thing yet, and as much as making love would be wonderful, it might make keeping on track that much harder. Reluctance warred with need as she pulled her mouth away. She so didn't want to stop this. But she had to if she was to be true to herself. Which she had to be. Or else she'd lose everything.

Dear Reader,

Vicki and Cole were first mentioned in *The Nurse's Twin Surprise* and I knew immediately I would write their story.

It's always hard for a couple when one of them spends a lot of time away from home for work. Add in the person keeping the home fires burning and trying to pretend life is perfect, and there can be sadness and disappointment with the relationship.

Growing up in Cairns, Vicki has always been surrounded by family, and to find herself alone in Sydney is hard, so when things go wrong, it's hard for her to keep going. She loves Cole, but he's not home enough.

Cole has a promise to keep before he can give Vicki all the time and attention he wants to. And now she's saying their marriage is over.

Read their story and see how they get through this quagmire that has become their relationship.

Cheers!

Sue MacKay

suemackayauthor@gmail.com
SueMacKay.co.nz

RECLAIMING HER
ARMY DOC HUSBAND

SUE MacKAY

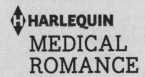

HARLEQUIN
MEDICAL
ROMANCE

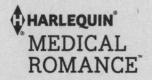

HARLEQUIN®
MEDICAL
ROMANCE™

Recycling programs
for this product may
not exist in your area.

ISBN-13: 978-1-335-14948-0

Reclaiming Her Army Doc Husband

Copyright © 2020 by Sue MacKay

Harlequin Enterprises ULC
22 Adelaide St. West, 40th Floor
Toronto, Ontario M5H 4E3, Canada
www.Harlequin.com

Printed in U.S.A.

Sue MacKay lives with her husband in New Zealand's beautiful Marlborough Sounds, with the water on her doorstep and the birds and the trees at her back door. It is the perfect setting to indulge her passions of entertaining friends by cooking them sumptuous meals, drinking fabulous wine, going for hill walks or kayaking around the bay—and, of course, writing stories.

Books by Sue MacKay

Harlequin Medical Romance

London Hospital Midwives
A Fling to Steal Her Heart

SOS Docs
Redeeming Her Brooding Surgeon

Baby Miracle in the ER
Surprise Twins for the Surgeon
ER Doc's Forever Gift
The Italian Surgeon's Secret Baby
Taking a Chance on the Single Dad
The Nurse's Twin Surprise

Visit the Author Profile page
at Harlequin.com for more titles.

Dedicated to my wonderful friend Vicki Rule, who has a fantastic shoe collection and is one of the kindest and strongest women I know.

CHAPTER ONE

'COLE, IT'S ME. I need to talk to you urgently. Please, sweetheart.' Vicki Halliday pressed her phone so hard against her ear it hurt. 'We've got a problem.'

She'd miscarried. Their baby was gone. Their dreams and excitement were over. Maybe her dream more than his. He'd seemed a little distant since learning about the pregnancy.

'Please leave a message after the beep and I'll get back to you as soon as possible,' her husband's strong, don't-mess-with-me voice intoned. Not the voice she adored, went to bed with to have sweet nothings whispered against her skin. Not the man she hugged and kissed in return because of the deep sexiness that was the love of her life.

She pressed 'off' and leaned forward over her knees, her hands clenched around the only link she had with her husband. Damn, how she missed him. Would give anything for him to be here so they could get through the loss of their baby together.

Not that there was anything unusual about his absence. Twelve months ago he hadn't been around when she'd had to have their spaniel Benji put down after a car had hit the beloved pet that had helped her through the lonely days when Cole was offshore. Neither had he been around two months later when her mother had been having chemo and Vicki had thought she would lose her too.

He *had* surprised her by turning up for her thirtieth birthday. One night of passion, then he was gone before she'd woken up. Gone without a word of when he'd see her next, without waking her to say he loved her. As always, he'd had to follow orders. Fair enough. He'd gone into the job willingly. But she hadn't. Now he was in East Timor with his army unit. Not here. Where he was needed the most. Where, for once, he could put his own needs aside and help her through this tragedy—together.

'Cole, you have to answer your phone pronto.'

In desperation she tapped his number again. Again heard his impersonal message.

The pain and despair combined to fling words out of her mouth with no thought of consequences. 'Just for once, answer your blasted phone, Cole Halliday. I've miscarried our baby,'

Vicki shrieked through a burst of pain. 'I've miscarried,' she repeated, quieter this time.

The words clogged her throat and she threw the phone onto the couch beside her as she sprawled lengthways in a wasted attempt to ease the ache in her abdomen. And her heart. 'This can't be happening,' Then again, why not? Nothing had gone right in their marriage for a while, so why would believing she'd see their pregnancy through to full term be any different? Except this time the pain was unbearable, and that wasn't the physical.

I've lost our baby.

'It's so unfair,' she cried through clenched jaws.

I think I've lost my husband, too.

'Still no answer?' Molly rubbed Vicki's back.

'Obviously not,' she vented at her friend, then instantly regretted it. None of this was Molly's fault. Molly had strapped her baby twins into the car and driven halfway across Sydney to pick her up the moment Vicki had said what was happening.

Also, as much as she wanted to, she couldn't really blame Cole for the fact she was losing their baby. But he should be here, cuddling her, or rubbing her back when it ached instead of Molly sharing her grief because it would be his, too. No matter how hard her friend tried, it wasn't the same as having the man she loved with her during this crisis, giving the emotional support he all too often failed on. Because he stood tall, he thought she could too.

Instead she was used to having a loving family at her side through everything, so these past years in Sydney away from them, and with Cole coming and going, had been hard. He didn't get it. Didn't understand how much she needed him to listen to her worries and take them on board. Like Molly was doing now. She dragged herself upright. 'Sorry, ignore me.'

'It's okay. I get it.'

'True.' If anyone did, Molly did. Years ago her friend's ex had put her through a horrific miscarriage via a fist to her stomach. For Molly, it had been the final straw in a violent marriage, and she'd left him for good. Eventually, she'd found happiness with Cole's best friend, Nathan.

'I only wish you weren't going through this.'

Vicki gave a sick sigh. Right this moment she struggled to find the strength to see it through without her man. 'You and me both.' All the excitement of having a baby, of believing that she and Cole would be a proper family with a child to nurture and love, had gone down the drain, almost literally. Angry tears burned down her cheeks. Her broken heart continued doing its job from under a weight of despair and sadness. She was a mixed bag of emotions, not one of them good. 'Cole's not here to see it. To hold my hand. To tell me silly stuff like I'll be all right. That we'll try again.' If he wanted to.

'Here.' A box of tissues appeared before her. 'He'll feel terrible when he gets your message.'

When he got it. Who knew exactly where he was and for how long? Not her. He never told her when he was going on a mission, or what happened on the forays the unit engaged in. Not that she wanted the details, they'd only give her more graphic nightmares worrying if he was safe.

'You reckon?' Vicki couldn't help the bitterness tainting her question. Was she being unfair? Selfish? Sure she was, but today she didn't care much. She needed Cole. Right here. Now. Not in another country looking out for people he didn't know. It was important to him, and some would say she was selfish, that other army wives coped with disasters.

To hell with them. Watching her mother, after her close shave with cancer, begin to understand how much she'd sacrificed for her family, Vicki had started realising she was going down the same track by forfeiting her own needs to keep Cole happy. She liked making others happy, or helping them get well. It was one reason she'd become a nurse. When she and Cole had got married her own dreams had gone on hold, but over the past year she'd begun resurrecting the idea of owning a nursing agency. Maybe she should've done it when Cole had first signed up and then perhaps she wouldn't be so at odds with him now.

She hadn't known where to start. It didn't come naturally. Cole didn't understand how important it was to her to create something for herself, so she'd vacillated between what she had and what she wanted. When she'd become pregnant, the future had become clearer—in a different direction. She would raise her child with all the love she was capable of, while still being there for Cole, at his side, loving him. Putting herself on the backburner. Just like her mother had done with her father, and now regretted.

Watching her mother blossom over the last months as she followed her artistic aspirations had been an eye-opener, and had made Vicki take a long look at herself. It was scary. Following through on her own dreams might mean losing Cole. If that happened, then maybe she'd fallen in love with the wrong man. *No*. She loved him so much, that wasn't possible.

Whatever the truth, all the hopes and plans and excitement of a family were now finished. Gone. Poof. No more. Through no fault of her own, or Cole's. Miscarriages happened—often. She just hadn't figured she'd be a statistic. Nei-

Molly wrapped her in a hug. 'I'm glad you called me.'

'So am I. It would've been an even longer day if I hadn't.'

She'd phoned in a panic when she'd realised what was happening and, while it wasn't essential she go to the emergency department, they'd agreed it was better if she got checked over at the hospital where she and Nathan worked and let him talk her through the medical details—which she knew from a nursing perspective—before Molly brought her back to their house.

She was so grateful for Molly's company, though it was hard when the babies cried, or needed feeding or changing. That was supposed to have been *her* future. If Cole had been around she wouldn't have needed anyone else to hold her, talk when she wanted a distraction, listen to her vent about how unfair life was. He would have understood everything.

Before heading outside, she picked up her phone to tap Cole's number, knowing he still didn't answer but needing to hear his voice.

'Sweetheart, answer me.'

'Sleave a message...'

She murmured 'off', tossed the phone aside. So message ing to listen to his voice. The message wasn't solely for her, it was generic. It sexy. She choked, the tears a ther had she'd started her pregnancy thinking how it might go wrong. That was unhealthy. Yet she was already grieving for her baby.

Where should she go from here? She could go back to work tomorrow, get on with living like nothing had happened, stiff upper lip and all that. It was a role she had played every time Cole had left her for another army excursion. Taking days off would only add to her loneliness. Her friends would be at work or, like Molly, busy with their little ones. To head home to the family in Cairns where she'd be wrapped in love and comfort would make it even harder to return to Sydney and the empty apartment at the end of her break.

Molly hadn't finished playing the diplomat. 'You know Cole will be gutted. He was so excited about the pregnancy, and he loves you to bits.'

'Then why do I come second to everything?' The army was like another wife, a more demanding one who had to be obeyed at all cost. Right from the start of their relationship Cole had warned her he was going to sign up after finishing his medical degree. Because she'd been so much in love she'd thought she'd manage as long as he was in her life. Going along with his plans without question made him happy.

Unfortunately, she hadn't *known* what living

alone while married really entailed. Hadn't understood the relentless loneliness when he was away for months on end. An isolation that encroached even when he was back in Sydney and they were sharing army digs. Sharing a bed, spending their days and nights together—when he wasn't working—was what she craved when he wasn't here and worked at making wonderful when he was.

Yet being a soldier wasn't like any regular job. Not even a medical registrar's frantically busy position had taken him away from her so much. Often lately, even when he was home with her, he wasn't really *with* her.

Regret for not getting on with the agency years ago hit hard. She'd have been busy, focused, not trying to fill in the empty hours. Deep down, she'd been hoping the baby would change everything, bring Cole home to her permanently so he'd share their lives beside her, not from a distance. *And* give her strength to revisit her plans. But her baby was gone. Raw agony slammed into her again. There was nothing to smile about.

'You're staying here with us tonight, no argument.' Molly locked her newly learned formidable gaze with hers, which was no doubt pathetically sad at the moment.

'You didn't used to be so bossy,' Vicki muttered through an overwhelming gratitude that she'd met this woman and they'd become firm friends.

'That's a yes, then.'

'Didn't think I had any choice.' She had nothing to hide from Molly. 'Okay, thank you. I don't want to go back to the apartment and stare at the walls while trying to absorb what's happened.' Yes, happened, as in no going back. No changing the outcome. The bleeding had begun sometime before she'd woken that morning and was all but done now, though the occasional painful cramps still underscored what had occurred. As if she needed reminding. The weight on her chest, the emptiness in her heart, the incessant tears—all tells of her loss. *Our loss.* Just because she hadn't spoken to Cole didn't mean his world hadn't irrevocably changed too.

She straightened up, swung her legs over the side of the couch. She needed to be doing something, not lying around waiting for the next hit from life. 'I'm going to walk to the end of the lawn and back.' Stop and stare out over the Tasman Sea from the clifftop, and draw up some strength to move forward.

'Want me to come with you? I can bring the baby monitor. It works from as far as the fence.'

Vicki shook her head. 'I'll be fine. You stay near those two cuties.' Her lip trembled.

Molly wrapped her in a hug. 'I'm glad you called me.'

'So am I. It would've been an even longer day if I hadn't.'

She'd phoned in a panic when she'd realised what was happening and, while it wasn't essential she go to the emergency department, they'd agreed it was better if she got checked over at the hospital where she and Nathan worked and let him talk her through the medical details— which she knew from a nursing perspective— before Molly brought her back to their house.

She was so grateful for Molly's company, though it was hard when the babies cried, or needed feeding or changing. That was supposed to have been *her* future. If Cole had been around she wouldn't have needed anyone else to hold her, talk when she wanted a distraction, listen to her vent about how unfair life was. He would have understood everything.

Before heading outside, she picked up her phone to tap Cole's number, knowing he still wouldn't answer but needing to hear his voice. 'Cole, sweetheart, answer me.'

'Please leave a message…'

She banged 'off', tossed the phone aside. So much for needing to listen to his voice. The message was not solely for her, it was generic. It wasn't special, or sexy. She choked, the tears a waterfall soaking into her crumpled tee shirt. 'Where the hell are you?' she yelled.

Nathan appeared in the doorway. 'Vicki? It's hard, that's what it is.' He crossed the room to hug her. 'Cole will call as soon as he can.'

'I know that. But it'll be too late.' She sniffed, soaked up some of her friend's warmth and leaned back to look directly at the man she'd known almost as long as she'd known Cole. 'I need him *now*.' Already the emptiness from losing her baby was taking over, more destructive because her husband wasn't here to share it, to console her, to let her comfort him. They could've cried together, held each other, got through the days ahead a little easier. 'I really do.'

'You'll get through this. You're tougher than you think.' Nathan squeezed tighter, then released her, a grim expression on his face.

Tough? Yes, she could be. But today she'd run out of tough. She wanted to be selfish for a while. Curling up in bed, pulling the covers over her head, and ignoring the world going on around her was a priority right now. Which was why she'd go outside for a few minutes. Acting tough? Sniff. *I suppose*. But, no, she really had had enough.

The phone rang. She stared at it. Was it Cole? No, it wouldn't be. Hope rose, fell, rose higher, like a wave in a storm. Reaching for the instrument, she picked it up, stared at the screen. Her heart soared. Cole. Pressing the button, she banged the phone against her ear. 'Hey, I'm sorry. So, so sorry.' Like it was her fault. Who knew? Maybe it was.

'Sweetheart, is it true?'

'Why wouldn't it be?' As if she'd make up something like that.

'I didn't want to believe your message. Are you all right? I hope you're not alone.'

Her eyes widened. Cole wasn't exactly spilling his heart with support and love. Was she all right? 'No, I'm not all right,' she snapped through her tears. 'I'm with Molly and Nathan, at their place,' she added.

'That's good. They'll take care of you.' He really was a barrel of comforting words.

'They can't replace you. It's your arms I long for. It's you I need to hug and cry with, not our friends.' Didn't he get it? They were a couple. They shared everything.

'Unfortunately, there's not a thing I can do about it. The CO won't let me go at the moment. There's a mission starting tomorrow we've been preparing for that requires everyone on board,' he explained. 'It will take all our resources to pull it off.'

'Cole, I've miscarried. I don't care about your

mission.' Had they drifted so far apart that they couldn't connect over this? She didn't want to believe that. She loved Cole more than anyone, anything. Yet nothing about their relationship felt safe any more. It was as though she lived in a dark box and only came out when he was back in Sydney, when it suited the army to let him have time off. He'd chosen to sign up, never really explaining why, always fobbing her off when she asked, which irked, but as usual she'd let it go rather than start an argument.

'Hang in there, sweetheart. I am getting out at the end of my contract.'

That's for ever.

She swallowed the bitter taste in her mouth. She'd have to find it within her to see out the days and weeks. 'Are you certain?' Because if he changed his mind she'd never cope. 'You don't always tell me everything.' There were things he never discussed, especially about his youth. Sometimes, when it got too much for him, he'd spill his anguish over some of the tragedies he'd seen with the army. She'd listen, try to console him, and he'd pull himself together. Once he'd told her she was the strongest woman he knew for taking him on. Maybe it had been Cole's love for her speaking, because she hadn't been that tough, though over the past year she'd tried to improve. Or so she'd thought. Today she was floundering.

'I'm telling you I'm leaving the army. I will not have a second crack at it. I've done what I set out to do. I want to be with you, Vicki. More than occasionally.'

Her heart swelled with love. That was what she'd waited to hear for so long.

'We just have to get through the next year.'

Her relief deflated like a pricked balloon at that reminder. It seemed so long. Time interspersed with occasional visits when they'd make love and laugh. Not a lot of talking happened, and then she'd go back to that box. 'Then what will you do?'

'It's too soon to decide.'

Once again he wasn't telling her anything. He must have been considering his next move. Cole didn't make major changes without thinking everything through thoroughly. Fresh pain engulfed her. Where was his love? Not in his voice or words. All hope of him comforting her was deflated; left her cold and drained.

Her mouth dried as she whispered, 'Cole, I don't think I can do this any more. I married to be with you, not the wife in the background, available whenever you have a few hours or days to spare. To me, marriage is about having you around whenever my world flips upside down.

To be there for you when yours goes haywire. To share everything.'

Oh, hell, what did she mean? Was she walking away from him? For good? Was that what she wanted? No, it wasn't. She loved him. But she couldn't continue with the way things were. It *was* only for another year, but then what? More Cole ideas she was supposed to fit in with? Her patience had gone from thin to non-existent. But? But could she leave Cole? Tough, remember? Lonely, remember? Alone, not lonely. Yeah. Lonely *and* alone.

'Vicki, don't say that.' Panic flared in his voice. 'Please, don't, sweetheart. I know you're going through hell right now, but I'm here for you. You know that.'

'No, you're not. You haven't been here anytime I've needed you.'

Stop it, Vicki.

This was a conversation for when they were together, not over a phone. Therein lay the problem. When would they be together again? 'The miscarriage is the last straw. I cannot live always waiting for you to show up. I need fixed plans to work towards, and to follow some of my dreams as well.'

'Wait, Vicki. We'll talk. I have to finish this duty. I don't know when I'll return to Sydney to see out my time but it will happen.'

'We'll talk? Over the phone? That's great when it's something as important as our future, as us. As losing our baby.' Tears flooded down her cheeks. 'I can't sit back and wait for you to come home for a face-to-face discussion. I need to see you *now*.'

'Sweetheart, you know that can't happen. It's impossible.'

'Exactly.' Life as she knew it was over. What she had to find out was how to make it unfold in the future. But not today. Today was raw enough without adding to the agony.

Cole winced as the line went dead. Vicki had hung up on him. After saying she doubted she could carry on with their marriage. Without talking about the miscarriage. A dull throbbing started behind his ribs. Vicki was the love of his life, his first reason for waking up every morning. She could not leave him. She didn't mean it. She was broken-hearted about their baby. That's what this was about. She was trying to cope in any way possible.

The pain in her voice had been like nothing he'd heard before, not even when her mother had been so ill no one had believed she'd pull through. Vicki's pain had got deeper and stronger as she'd talked, adding to his guilt, creating a sense of failure for not being there with her.

She needed him. More than anyone. And there was nothing he could do about it. His own pain scudded across his lips in a sigh. Once again he'd hurt one of the most important people in his life.

We've lost our baby.

Sharp agony squeezed hard, taking away his ability to breathe. Why was he here, and not with Vicki?

He had chosen this life to meet a promise he had made to his mother when he was seventeen. Along with two close mates and his girlfriend, he'd been accused of the theft of thousands of dollars from a local charity after a fundraising event. Not even his parents had believed him when he'd said he knew nothing about the robbery. All he did remember was the four of them going to the local park late that night where he'd had two beers while cuddling with his girlfriend. The next thing he recalled was waking up alone in his car outside his family's home.

Many months later, one of his mates had confessed that the girlfriend had put a date drug in Cole's beer to make him sleep, then had taken his car keys and driven herself and the other two guys to the charity building to steal the money.

The shame of not being aware of what had gone on around him that night and how easily he'd been used hadn't left him. Only his granddad had stood by him, saying what had happened had changed his life for ever, but he mustn't let it ruin his future. He had loved him for that more than anything. His mother had lost most of her friends and become stressed and anxious. His father, a criminal lawyer, had hidden behind his work, putting in ever-increasing hours and staying away from home. Even when they'd finally admitted they'd been wrong, his family had never returned to being their easy, loving selves. They'd let him down.

As I have Vicki.

His gut clenched.

We've lost our baby. I'm not there for Vicki.

But he had to be here. It was the promise he'd made to his mother before he'd been exonerated and she'd lain dying in ICU after a massive heart attack. Desperate for her to live, he'd have promised the moon if it would've helped. Instead he'd said he'd make her proud by joining the army after he'd become a doctor, which had always been his aspiration. Granddad had been a highly decorated soldier, and Cole had also wanted to show him he was worthy of his belief in his grandson.

That night his mother had passed away, never to see him fulfil his promise, leaving him with a load of remorse nothing would shake. Had the stress from what had happened caused her death? The guilt and shame had stuck to him like glue.

And now this. The baby was gone. Unbelievable. Even to his doctor's brain it didn't make sense. It was so unfair. Cole couldn't find any words to describe his feelings at this moment. In trying to do right by his mother and granddad, he'd let his wife down so much. If only he had a red cape and could fly to her side, hug her, kiss her, promise they'd make it through this latest tragedy—together.

His life had become compartmentalised after he'd been exonerated. Adelaide—the good, bad and downright ugly. Sydney—adulthood, medicine, new friends. Vicki. The army—meeting his promise. Vicki. His love. He groaned. Vicki. What he wouldn't give to be with her. Right from the beginning of their relationship it had been good having someone believe in him, love him, without having to expose the frankly awful time of his past. Though deep, deep down lay a seed of doubt about that decision not to tell her. But he hadn't wanted to bring the past into the future with her.

Nathan was the only person he'd told the whole truth to when he'd demanded to know why they couldn't go to Adelaide for a break and get together with Cole's friends from school days. Because Nathan held nothing back from him, he'd finally explained. It had been a test of their friendship, one that had never faltered.

Yet he still hadn't found the courage to tell Vicki. She was a fresh start he hadn't wanted to taint with the past. She was the precious jewel in his life. He loved her so much sometimes it was almost too much, made him fear he couldn't get enough of her. Yet here he was in East Timor while she was back in Sydney, needing him desperately.

She's thinking about leaving you.

She couldn't. He'd talk to her as soon as he returned to base. She was hurting. Big time. He understood. But leave him? No. She didn't mean it. She needed time to come to terms with the miscarriage.

Which is why I should be with her, not here.

There wasn't anything he could do about it. Except go AWOL, and the consequences of that would be worse. So he'd phone every day. It wouldn't be enough, but it was all he could offer. It would help him to get through this ragged pain caused by the miscarriage. He'd signed up for the army without a backward glance, ignoring the sadness in her eyes, only saying it was a promise he owed. Whenever he'd been home and she'd hinted that it was getting lonely living in their apartment in the middle of such a large city, he'd worked hard to put a smile back on her face and made love to her so she knew he was on her side. And every time he'd gone away *again*, following orders, using them as an excuse for the life he was living. He'd been utterly selfish.

As he and the men headed back to barracks from their last training exercise before tomorrow's job, he stared out at the passing scenery of never-ending dirt and dust and crowds of people trying to get by in this area, trying to absorb everything Vicki had said, failing to ignore the ache under his ribs. The miscarriage. Her pain. The life he'd chosen to follow that kept him away from her. The army was like nothing he'd ever known. With the way everyone had to fall into step, dress the same, eat the same, be prepared for anything horrific any time, he didn't enjoy the life, but once he'd fulfilled his promise he'd be able to get on with the next phase of his life without looking back.

The marriage vows he'd made to Vicki needed acknowledgement. To love and cherish and be there always, through the wonderful and the awful.

Vicki, I am so bloody sorry. We've lost our baby and you need me. I need you.

He'd signed up for that, too. Vicki was his future, the army the final nail in his past.

His stomach tightened into a painful ball.

Their baby was gone. It had been amazing to learn he was going to be a dad. He'd been stoked, couldn't wait for it to be born. He'd already imagined playing football, going fishing, having family picnics at the beach with his son or daughter. Family was what it was all about. A loving, caring, believing family. And Vicki, the most amazing woman to have kids with. Now it wasn't happening.

'You okay, Captain?' The driver of their truck had turned to look at him as they drove along the main road out of a village.

No. I've never felt worse.

'All good,' he lied through gritted teeth. Something large and dark hurtled across the road directly at them. A laden ute. 'Look out, soldier,' he snapped.

The driver swore as he wrenched their lumbering vehicle to the right. His reaction might've been fast but the other vehicle was faster.

Cole's butt left the seat, his head punched through the windscreen. Fear tightened his belly. Not now. Not when he needed to be at home. His body was airborne. Air stalled in his lungs. Landing was going to hurt. Or worse, he thought. His fingers gripped his phone as though his life depended on it.

Vicki! I love you. Wait for me.

CHAPTER TWO

'JACK, BEHAVE. Water will soak that moonboot if you don't hurry up and get in the car,' Vicki growled at the man she was trying to help into the passenger seat while he fiddled with the window button, opening and closing the window.

The umbrella she held over them both wasn't working. Water had found its way through the back of her shirt. At this rate, by the time she returned inside the medical centre she'd be soaked.

'You're worse than most toddlers I've worked with.'

'I was one once,' the middle-aged man grunted, and finally sank onto the seat and lifted his damaged leg inside. 'Quite the nuisance, I've been told.'

'You don't have to sound proud of it. You're not doing yourself any favours thinking you're one of the world's heroes who has to be out amongst it all the time.' Vicki dredged up a smile for the fireman who was temporarily off work thanks to having rolled a quad bike down a slope on his rural property a couple of weeks previously. 'You've got to take things easy.'

'Boring,' Jack mock-yawned.

'You think?' She shook her head in admonishment at her brother's friend, before nodding to his wife. 'Try and keep him out of mischief until those ribs and fractured thigh have had time to knit.'

'Give me something easy to do.' Barbara laughed. 'The moment I turn my back he'll be heading for his shed and the other quad bike.'

'I figured.' She shrugged. 'Men, eh?' Hell, she missed hers so much she hardly slept at night after following through on her decision to walk away from her marriage. It hadn't been easy. When she hadn't heard from Cole for more than a week after the miscarriage she'd closed in on herself and tried to deal with the agony of losing their baby alone.

Quitting her job at the hospital, unable to stand the sympathy in everyone's eyes whenever she turned up at work, she'd packed up the apartment and headed north to Cairns and her family, to be surrounded in their care. And the tears kept on coming. She'd never known it was possible to bawl her eyes out so much. There shouldn't be that much fluid in a person's body.

Still the agony hadn't abated. Not for her baby or her marriage.

Nothing filled the void that had once been her excitement over being pregnant. Or the empty air between her and Cole. When he'd finally begun phoning, their conversations had been stilted, and the silences, longer every time, had become full of all the things neither seemed able to voice. Eventually, she'd told him they were over and had gone to stay with her sister in London while she made decisions about the future. As if she could decide with all the distressing emotions tugging at her heart.

Cole had gone quiet again. As in not a word by phone or email. The hurt grew. It was so typical of him not to talk about the important stuff. It was the main reason she'd left him. There'd be no more waiting around, ready to put everything on hold whenever he came home, and then go back to a kind of single life when he left again. That was over. Even when he got out of the army she'd still be that wife, trying to keep him happy all the time and putting herself on hold for the foreseeable future. Like her mum had done, first for her dad and then for her and her siblings.

Warmth stole through Vicki as she remembered presenting Mum with an easel and painting equipment. Mum's shock, the delight followed by excitement had said it all.

'You wouldn't want a wuss for a husband.' Jack grinned at Barbara around a groan as he settled further onto the seat.

Vicki shivered. *She* hadn't had one either. Cole was a tough guy who never showed pain or hurt. Too much so. If only he could've relented a little and stopped being so strong, they might not be about to spend the weekend together, finalising the dissolution of their marriage. His attitude was a mask he didn't drop even for her. Which wasn't right.

There weren't supposed to be any secrets between them, yet more and more she'd started seeing there were. He'd never explained why he'd needed to sign up for the military, just muttered something about keeping a promise. She'd asked for more information—often—and been fobbed off every time.

But were they really over? It felt like it. It had done for months, if not longer, when she thought about how she hadn't recognised the loneliness and need to fill her time with anything for what it really was.

The recent months spent mostly travelling while trying to side-track herself from the mess that had become her life hadn't been easy but at least now she was working to find her feet again, beginning with making the goal of her own nursing agency a reality. The idea held the promise of something exciting, something to hold onto and gain strength from her efforts.

Her fingers clenched the umbrella. First there was the weekend to get through. Time with Cole. How would she cope? Seeing him, breathing in his smell, being stuck in the house together—the thought had her heart racing already. As long as they didn't get angry at each other or upset one another too much. Tears were already threatening, and he wasn't due yet.

'See you on Monday when I bring Jack back to have his dressings changed.' Barbara revved the engine, then stuck her head out the window. 'If you feel like a coffee any time, just drop in.'

'Thanks. I might do that when I've run out of ways to annoy Damon.' Her older brother was a fireman at the same station as Jack, and everyone there had been super-friendly since she'd arrived back in Cairns from London three weeks ago.

Her other brother, Phil, was a local cop, and he too seemed intent on keeping an eye on her by including her in every social event he went to—usually for a pint at the pub. She loved them both, but they could be a little suffocating.

With Cole coming, their protective instincts were on high alert. In the past she'd relished their support, but now she needed to do this without them interfering. Her spine *was* getting straighter, tougher.

Ducking under the overhang at the medical centre entrance, she saw a taxi pull up over the road. She had two patients to go before she packed it in for the weekend and headed to the airport to wait for Cole. Scratching her palms, she swallowed hard. Air slowly seeped from her lungs. Nothing about the weekend was going to be easy.

It wouldn't take forty-eight hours to come to an arrangement about whether to sell the Sydney apartment or get Cole to buy her out. That was the sum of their marriage now. Her stomach had been a tight ball all day, and she hadn't eaten a thing, replacing food with endless mugs of coffee, and now was so jittery her teeth clacked.

Closing the umbrella, she shook the water off before dropping it into the tall pot standing in the corner. Despite the incessant monsoon rain the air was still warm and humid. There was nothing like Queensland temperatures to make her feel right at home again. Except she wasn't. These past weeks she'd been unsettled about whether to stay here permanently or return to Sydney and her friends down there. She presumed Cole would live there once he returned to civilian life, which held her back on that choice.

If—when—they divorced she'd want to live somewhere without all the memories. Sometimes, in the middle of the night, she'd admit she wanted to be near him. But that wasn't being strong. And strong was what she had to be, otherwise why go through this agony of finishing her marriage to the man she'd given her heart to?

Cole was out of the army early. He hadn't said why. Typical. Her heart thumped hard. Despite everything she'd said in the brief phone conversations in the past months, he still hadn't recognised how much she needed to share his life, to understand his thinking; not to be standing on the sidelines, waiting for him to give her some attention.

Footsteps on the path.

Her skin prickled. No, it was too early. Cole's flight from Sydney wasn't due for three hours. The goosebumps tightened, the hairs on the back of her neck lifted. She wasn't ready to confront him, needed more time to get her game face on. Although, she had to admit it, she'd never be ready. But—but this weekend wasn't going to go away without her spending time with Cole. Only one person turned her into a blithering wreck just by being near him. He was here.

Another wet step. 'Hello, Vicki.' Two words, soft, endearing, and full of memories that threatened to make those tears spill. Blink, blink. She loved that voice, heard it in her sleep, held it to her whenever she needed her man. Every day and night. Thump-thump, banged her heart.

Be strong.

Which was easier said than done.

'Cole.' That taxi must've dropped him off. 'Hello,' she muttered through suddenly dry lips.

The rate of her heart lifted. The ends of her fingers tingled. Cole. The man she adored. The man she had to hold out on for a more secure future. The man she'd once done anything to make happy, and now couldn't. *Wouldn't.* Her breathing went out of whack.

'Vicki.' He paused, waited, finally asked, 'How are you?'

He had to ask? The brave face slipped on. She didn't bother forcing a smile. Straightening her back, she slowly pivoted around on her heels to stare at her handsome husband. Except— The ground moved beneath her feet. Putting her hands out for balance, she struggled to stay upright. 'Cole?' She gasped. This was all wrong. 'What's happened? Are you all right?' Stupid question. He looked terrible. Worse than terrible. 'Obviously not.' Her instinct was to rush to him, wind her arms around that body she knew so well—not like this, she didn't—and never let go. To take away his pain, make him better.

We're over, remember?

She drew in air, clamped down on her emotions, clenched her hands at her sides, and remained fixed to the spot. Not that her feet could've lifted off the porch. They were as heavy as rocks. Studying him, her heart pounded harder, the tingling in her fingers tightened. He was far too thin. There were lines on his face that hadn't been there before. When he stepped closer his left leg dragged. There was fierce concentration on that lined, grey face, as though he was determined she wouldn't see how much it hurt to move. But there was no hiding the pain reflected in his eyes. 'Cole?' she whispered through pain of a different kind. 'Please tell me you're all right.' Please, please.

'Vicki. I'm all right.' Two more steps and he stood before her, looking stunned. Lifting his arms as though he was going to hug her, he hesitated, dropped his hands to his sides. 'Hello, sweet—' He stopped, staring at her, swallowing non-stop. 'Damn,' he muttered.

Vicki jerked backwards, away from his tempting body. Tension sparked between them like forked lightning. Anxiety blindsided her. She couldn't do this. He'd nearly called her sweetheart. As normal, as though nothing was wrong.

I love him. Totally. Nothing has changed.

Her heart was coming out of her chest, her head spinning out of control.

I love him as much as ever.

Forget all the doubts since the miscarriage. Forget her own needs. Cole meant everything to her. Memories of him holding her, his hands strong, and warm, and, well, right. They fitted her. Slowly, she raised her head to gaze into his dark blue eyes.

I love you.

Had she said that out loud? He hadn't reacted, so hopefully she hadn't. The moment for telling him would never come if they didn't reach some understanding. They had to. He meant everything to her, was her life, the future.

Fight for what you want.

This weekend was about finishing their relationship, or possibly getting back together with different ideas of how to go ahead.

She froze, one muscle at a time. Gritted her teeth to keep words back. Words like, 'Hello, darling, I've missed you so much'. She wasn't going to be that woman again. Had no intention of returning to being the woman who was more concerned about keeping Cole happy before all else. She would eventually shrivel inside, turn bitter, or unhappy and sad as her mother had become before she'd woken up to what she needed to do. It was time to fight for herself, not give in to this gripping love.

Remaining still, she denied the warmth and longing warring in her veins. Fought the desire to touch Cole, to lean in against that altered yet familiar body. To let him hug her tight and close. To hug him back like there was no tomorrow. But there was. Give in now and she might as well walk down the drive and go back to Sydney with him tonight, no conversations, no plans or changes made. Forget her hopes for the future.

'You're early.'

Lame, Vicki. But she was fighting for survival. Anything went.

'I didn't want this weather bomb to prevent me making it to Cairns so I changed my flight.' His gaze bored into her with a hunger she hadn't expected since their infrequent phone discussions had been so awkward.

It was good to see his reaction; despite everything, it warmed her throughout. It had to mean there was hope. What was she hoping for? A lightning bolt moment where Cole understood what she needed? After all these years?

'I could not miss seeing you for anything,' he added.

Now Cole stood before her, she realised she'd been holding her breath for days in case he changed his mind about coming. Not that he would've. That wasn't his way. But, still, their relationship was unrecognisable. They had to do this, sort out everything before they could move on separately. Not together. He'd wouldn't have changed that much. Nausea rose.

Give in, carry on being the pleaser you're so good at being. Kiss him, hug him. Buy a ticket on the next flight to Sydney. Make him happy.

No. She mustn't. Because eventually something would happen to drive a wedge between them again, or she'd sink into an abyss where she'd given up on herself. But she still loved Cole. There was no denying that. Which only made everything so much harder. 'I've still got nearly an hour before finishing up here.'

He nodded curtly, wincing as he shrugged his shoulder where a small pack hung against his back. Like it hurt having any weight pulling at him.

What had happened? 'Cole?' His name slipped across her lips before she could stop it. 'What—?'

He cut her off. 'Not now. I'll wait down the road at the pub.'

Nothing had changed. 'No. Tell me now.'

He shook his head as though clearing something away. Those piercing eyes she knew so well were filled with a pain she'd never seen before. They locked onto her, sending shivers of excitement right down to her damp toes. Damn him. 'Vicki, seeing you is the best thing to happen for a long time.'

As she made to stop him saying anything more that might undermine her determination to keep him at a distance she once more had to fight the urge to throw herself at him and hang on tight. As usual he'd deliberately diverted her from her question. Nothing new there.

Cole held up his hand. 'Hear me out.' Then he couldn't continue. Vicki, his beautiful wife, stood there, the battle going on in her head showing through her eyes and on her face. All he could think was, *I love you.* Nothing else mattered. He loved Vicki. He always had and always would.

Something like relief floored him. His love hadn't changed, was as deep, as strong, as ever. Not that there'd been any doubts, but *knowing* helped, shoved away some of the dread that getting together might make matters worse, not better. Over the days leading up to this moment he'd despaired that they mightn't talk, wouldn't resolve anything.

So tell her how you feel.

He opened his mouth. Closed it. Last time he'd said it over the phone she'd gone quiet, then said she had to go and hung up.

He found his voice. 'We have a lot to sort out,

and none of it's going to be easy, but I've missed you badly. More than ever. Seeing you tips me sideways.' And upside down, all around. He was not giving up without a fight. A hard one. With everything he had.

He'd started and was close to getting a job that involved staying in one place for the foreseeable future, which meant they could buy a house and settle down in Sydney. Try again for a baby. First he owed Vicki an apology. He'd given it more than once over the phone but face to face would go a lot further. She'd see his how genuine he was, not hear it over a bad phone connection.

'Cole, you're not making this any easier.'

She was definitely holding back, whereas he'd blurted out how he felt. He didn't do blurting. His gut churned. She hadn't reacted positively to being told he'd missed her. Were they really at an impasse? Please, not that. He hadn't said the three most important words. Should he? Would that break the barriers Vicki was clinging onto? Or would it put her on alert, make her warier than she already was? Because she was fighting to remain cautious. It showed in her rapid blinking, in the way the tip of her tongue poked over her lip.

He had to slow down. 'We've waited months to talk properly. We can wait a little longer. I'd rather be some place with just you, not out front of a medical practice. It feels rather surreal.'

'You can start by telling me why you're limping.'

This persistence was new, putting him on alert. He was in for a verbal hiding. And not as prepared as he needed to be. 'All in good time,' he said too forcefully, and suffered an unhappy glare coming straight back at him.

So they'd talk about whatever Cole chose, when he chose. 'How normal,' she muttered under her breath. From the moment she had sensed his presence she'd been struggling to stay grounded. Her head pounded in time with her heart. Parts of her body alternated between hot and chilled. This was the man she'd sworn to love for ever. It would be too easy to tell him nothing had changed, and then slip her hand in his and ask him to take her away, to forgive her for standing up for herself. But do that and she gave up *everything*. She'd go back to fitting in with his choices, ignoring her own. So... Deep breath.

'You're right. We will talk later. About everything.' Turning away, she tried to deny the ache in his eyes, worked hard at pretending this would all work out fine. Because it wouldn't. Cole loved her. She'd never doubted that. The problem was that it was on his terms, which he didn't recognise, and so she had to fight for her own.

That moment the rain became a torrent, pouring out of the sky as though a massive bucket had been tipped over the medical centre.

Turning back, she tried not to stare at Cole with hunger, or study the adorable face that followed her to sleep every night; tried to deny the heat unfurling in her belly. 'You'd better come inside while I finish up. You'll drown trying to reach the pub.' Cole was right before her, and she couldn't leap into his arms for fear of never stepping out of them again. She'd missed him so much it hurt with every breath. Somehow she was managing to hold back, fighting against herself for herself. 'Come in.'

'Thanks.' He stepped up behind her, putting all her senses on alert, making her skin tingle with a familiar need.

Pushing open the door, she quickly stepped inside and surprised herself by smiling. This was a temporary job; filling in for a nurse on her final month of maternity leave. She was in familiar territory, with family and friends to call on when everything got on top of her. Since starting to look into start-up plans, the reality of owning and managing an agency hit hard at unguarded moments. This being strong didn't come naturally. Doubts crept in. Was it worth giving up her marriage to own a business? She'd lost count of how many times she'd told herself that wasn't what this was all about, that she was looking out for herself. And Cole, if he accepted what she was doing. Because if she was happier then surely he would be too.

One of the practice doctors approached.

'Vicki, I've been listening in on the emergency frequency. There's flooding north of the city, nothing major at the moment, but who knows what'll happen if this rain continues to get heavier over the coming hours, as it's forecast to do.' Joe paused and glanced behind her.

She turned to make the introductions. 'This is my...' *Stop. Start again.* 'Cole Halliday—Joe Burrows.'

Grief flared in Cole's eyes, blinked away as he reached to shake hands with her current boss. 'Pleased to meet you. I got here just in time. They were talking about closing the airport when my flight landed.'

Joe nodded. 'I'm not surprised. The reports are getting worse by the hour.' He looked to her. 'You'd better get home while you can, otherwise you might find yourselves holed up somewhere in town.'

At least then they wouldn't be stuck in the house, just the two of them, trying to be friendly while working through the problems they faced.

Though hotel rooms weren't known for their spaciousness. Better the house. More rooms.

'I've still got two patients to come.' It wouldn't be fair to leave someone else to cover for her when everyone was anxious to go home as soon as they could.

'I'll see to them. If they turn up. The cancellations have escalated since lunch time.'

She couldn't find it in her to argue. 'Right, thanks. It'll be a slow trip as it is. Jack said more people than usual were heading out of town when he and Barbara came in. The schools closed at midday.' She couldn't put off spending time alone with Cole any longer. Did she really want to? In all honesty, no. The time had arrived to talk and make some decisions. 'I'll grab my gear.'

'Take one of the emergency kits in case you're needed to help someone at Palm Beach,' Joe said, before turning to Cole. 'You're a doctor, aren't you?'

'Yes, I am, so no issues with administering drugs if required should we get called to an emergency.'

'Great. If there's an accident it might be a problem for emergency services to reach the scene in this weather.'

'There were a lot of frustrated drivers doing

some damned silly things on the road in from the airport so anything's likely.'

Vicki interrupted the men. They were getting comfortable with each other. She didn't want that. This was her territory and Cole getting cosy only made it harder to keep him at arm's length. 'No need to take a kit from here. Dad's got a full drugs cabinet and the storeroom was topped up with everything you could think of before he and Mum left on their road trip.' These days her dad ran a small clinic at home when he wasn't tripping around in the campervan with Mum so she could take numerous photos for the paintings she hoped would re-establish herself as an artist. Right now they were in Western Australia. 'Keep yours here in case it's needed elsewhere.'

She rushed to the staffroom for her bag, said goodbye to the women in the office, and called to Cole. 'This way. Thanks for this, Joe.' Despite the tension in her stomach knotting tighter and tighter with each passing minute, she was grateful to him. To be stuck in town wouldn't be comfortable.

They dashed to her car, leapt in and slammed the doors, clothes soaked through in those few seconds. 'At least it's not cold,' she muttered. Inside and outside her pulsing body.

'How did you cope with the northern winter? I've seen pictures of England and Europe in blizzards and snowstorms. It's not exactly enticing to a Queenslander.' Cole adjusted the seat to give his long legs as much space as possible and clipped his seat belt in place.

If she hadn't been watching she'd have missed the tightening of his mouth as he shifted his left leg. What had happened? she asked herself again. Something terrible, by the way he looked and moved. Something more than a simple accident.

He hadn't mentioned anything during any of their infrequent phone conversations either. Anger started to boil at being left out of the loop—and his refusal to talk when she'd asked. She swallowed hard, forced it down. She'd demand answers when they were at home and she could watch his face. Right now she had to focus on *getting* home, and keeping the disturbing subjects on hold. 'You know me and any temperature below twenty degrees. Julie took me shopping for thick jackets and thermal tops the day I arrived in London.'

'How's Julie? Still enjoying living over there?' Cole and her sister had always got along, though now Julie was backing her determination to work out what she truly wanted with her future.

And her mother was setting a great example of being true to herself, even if it was thirty-five years late, by painting as though there were years of pictures stored in her mind waiting to be put on canvas. She was so happy and healthy. Dad was a different man too now that he understood there was more to gain than lose by supporting his wife in her endeavours. What were the chances of Cole doing the same if she explained again, more thoroughly? This time with more emphasis on how she'd still always be there for and with him.

'Julie loves London. If the company can arrange her a permanent work visa she intends staying on and buying an apartment. She's met a guy who might be the one.' She was head over heels and had still taken a month off work to go away with Vicki to Europe, leaving her boyfriend behind. Setting an example of how a relationship should not be about one person keeping the other happy all the time. That was her sister.

Their brothers had always kept an eye on them both, too, even more so on Vicki lately. They meant well, but nowadays she preferred making her own decisions, right or wrong. It gave her a sense of self-worth. In a way their loving stifled her, and could explain why she'd fallen in line with Cole right from the beginning. They all meant well. It didn't mean they were right.

'What did you think of the countries you visited in Europe? Would you go back again? In the summer?'

'Maybe one day.' She far preferred melting in Queensland's humidity and heat any day. 'I'd like to return to France and Italy. Four weeks was nowhere near long enough. We barely got started. During my month in London I took short trips all over the north of England and Wales when Julie was at work, and at the weekends she showed me around London and the South.'

'You never once mentioned wanting to go over there.' Was that annoyance in his voice?

Too bad. When she'd needed to get away from Sydney it had been an instinctive reaction to head home but for the first time it hadn't felt right. Everyone had wanted to tell her what to do. Julie said she had to make her own choices, and supported her without overwhelming her. 'I really went to spend time with Julie. I'd have gone wherever she was.'

'Within reason, I hope.'

'No war zones, for sure.' Leaning over the steering wheel, she peered through the river running down her windscreen where the wipers were on full speed and not achieving a lot. 'This is crazy.' So was the way longing for Cole kept catching at her. It was diverting her from what this weekend was about.

'At least there's not much traffic about any more.'

He was right. 'Most of the shops are closed.'

'Is there anything we need to get?'

'No. I did the groceries last night.' Got in extra beer and wine in case the going got too awkward. 'You're on cooking the steak.' He was a dab hand at getting the sirloin perfectly medium rare.

'I figured.' Though still guarded, his voice had lightened.

Getting closer to old times. She didn't want that. It was a slippery path. Her head thudded. Tears threatened.

Don't cry.

Then she'd need wipers on her eyeballs. She needed to get angry, not sad. No. Neither option was wise. Anger led to lack of control and that was one thing she couldn't afford to lose over the coming days. If only she could give in and pull over to the kerbside and wrap her arms around Cole and kiss him, long and deep, and filled with the love she had to deny. If only. A kiss might fix everything. Or nothing. But giving it a go would ease the tightness brought on by not throwing herself at him the moment he'd arrived at the medical centre as she'd always done in the past.

The desire became an ache in her heart,

throughout her body. For the first time ever they wouldn't be making love the moment they charged into the house. Or kissing like their lives depended on feeling, tasting, pressing their mouths together. What had she done? Why hadn't she found the patience to wait until he returned from East Timor before she changed everything? Then she could've kissed him and wound her arms and legs around him, and shown how much she loved him all over again.

And nothing would've changed.

True. She'd started something there was no going back on. Fear hit her. What if this really was the end of everything between them? It was all very well telling herself she was doing the right thing and that they might be finished as a result, but Cole was her other half. She loved him, needed and wanted him.

And I can't go back to being at his beck and call.

Her foot pressed harder on the accelerator and the car shot forward. She braked sharply, and the wheels skidded on the wet tarmac.

'Take it easy,' Cole snapped. On his thighs, his hands were clenched, while his whole body was rigid.

What was that about? Her driving hadn't been dangerous, just a little abrupt.

'Slow down.'

She didn't reply for fear of shouting that it was impossible to take any damned thing easy with him sitting beside her, sharing the air, diverting her from what she should be concentrating on. Instead she focused on driving carefully through the numerous massive puddles covering the road at regular intervals, and hoped fervently that they got through to Palm Beach, while swallowing the longing and disappointment filling her. With every kilometre she drove her stomach grew harder, tighter, filling with stress over resolving everything in a way that worked for both of them, and fear that they never would.

'Dad sends his love.' Cole broke the tightening silence. Unable to cope any more?

Did Conrad know she'd left Cole? She should've kept in touch since the miscarriage but it was difficult. He was Cole's father first and foremost. 'I phoned Conrad about the miscarriage. He was very upset, and supportive.'

Beside Vicki, Cole stared out the window, his fingers tapping a rhythm on his thighs as he recalled the day his dad had called to say Vicki had phoned about the miscarriage.

'You should tell her, son.'

His father's words had drummed inside Cole's head as he'd lain on his hospital bed in Darwin. 'Easy to say, Dad.'

'She has a right to know.' Dad hadn't given up. At least he'd promised not to talk to Vicki about Cole's accident until Cole had broached the subject first.

And that hadn't happened in a hurry. He hadn't been able to tell her until he'd known for certain he would walk again.

'Yes, she does. When I'm ready.'

He hadn't wanted to give her the chance to fly up to Darwin and see him attached to more medical equipment than he'd ever seen on any patient. It hadn't been the tubes that had worried him. It had been the reason for them. Not the splenectomy, or the three fractures to his left leg. It had been the pain in his back. The spinal damage was a concern, his orthopaedic surgeon had said. A downright nightmare, Cole had thought.

What if he never walked again? Until he could know for sure he would be able to get up and look after himself, he would not lay his problems at Vicki's feet. He had not wanted her taking him back because he was seriously injured. He couldn't have cope with that humiliation.

'She's got enough problems already.'

Neither could he have expected Vick to rush to his side when he hadn't been able to go to her, even before that vehicle had driven into the army truck. Not when she'd told him she couldn't take any more.

'You take care, son. I'll call again tomorrow.' His dad's voice had broken and he'd hung up before Cole could say any more.

'Damn it.' Cole had stared some more at the ceiling he'd been getting to know too well. 'I seem to have made a habit of upsetting those nearest and dearest without even trying.' Should he call Vicki and talk about that dreadful day? She wasn't going to happy whenever she learnt about it, which was a given, so he might as well wait until he was up on his feet. Because he would walk again. He *would*.

But what he wouldn't have given to have had the love of his life there with him; to hold her hand, feel her lips on his. Just to talk about them, the miscarriage, their future. A future they wouldn't have any more if she had meant what she'd said.

Giving in to the relentless agony in his heart, he had picked up the phone and hit the speed dial for Vicki. 'Hi, sweetheart. How are you today?'

'Much the same.' Her voice had had the familiar flatness he'd heard during the few conversations they'd had over the previous week. 'What about you?' It hadn't sounded like she even cared.

Resentment had risen. There he had been, incapacitated, in pain, afraid he might not walk again despite his determination he would, and she had been in a fog all of her own.

'Just great, thanks,' he had snapped.

'That's good. Did you want to talk about anything in particular?'

He hadn't even been able to wind her up, she had been so down. The Vicki of old would've bitten his head off for the way he'd just spoken. 'Yes, us.'

Her sigh had resonated through the ether. 'Oh.'

Guilt had fought with a sense of loss and of being let down. 'What do you expect, Vicki? That I'm going to let you walk away without a fight?'

'I don't know what to think about anything at the moment, Cole. Losing the baby dominates my thoughts. I feel so sad, it's unbearable. It makes me feel useless.' The most emotion he'd heard from her since she'd told him she'd lost the baby had come at him.

He had let her down. Big time. He had known it. The guilt wouldn't let up. And yet what was he supposed to have done, even if he hadn't ended up in hospital, fighting for his life? 'It's going to take time, sweetheart.' All he had wanted was a little understanding that he couldn't always do as she needed, that the army was in charge.

Tell her where you are. Let her come to you.

It had been so tempting. As his mouth had opened, he'd heard, 'That's all just about everyone says.' Back to the flat tone. 'I didn't expect it from you, Cole.'

He'd got it wrong again. 'I'm sorry. I'm at a loss for words.' A hug would have gone a long way further, but wouldn't happening any time soon. The next day he would have to demand to be allowed to try and sit up and put his feet on the floor. The next day he would have to start getting his life sorted so he could work at making Vicki happy again. If she'd let him.

CHAPTER THREE

'IDIOT! WATCH WHERE you're going.'

Vicki's raised voice interrupted Cole's thoughts.

He looked around, saw a car skidding on the wet surface at the traffic lights ahead. 'Going too fast?'

'Definitely.' Vicki swore, braked slowly as she pulled to the side of the road. 'What the—?'

A kid on a skateboard shot across the road out of control, directly into the path of a car coming the other way.

Cole held his breath, watching with horror.

The board flicked sideways, throwing the boy in the other direction, where he landed heavily against the kerb. The approaching car skidded to a stop less than a metre from the boy.

'Phew.' Air rushed out of Vicki's mouth. 'That was close.

'It sure was.' Cole was already clambering out of her vehicle. 'Better make sure he's all right.'

The kid was lying in water, looking stunned. 'What happened?'

He squatted down. 'You lost control. What did you think you were doing out on the road?' Did he not know how dangerous his actions had been?

'It's cool, skating in the water.' The boy moved, tried to sit up and let out a yelp. 'That hurts.'

'Where?'

'My arm.' The left one was at an odd angle.

'Let me look. I'm a doctor.'

Vicki joined them. 'I'll help you sit up. What's your name?'

'Evan. Is my arm broken?'

'Could be,' Cole replied as he felt gently along the already swelling forearm. 'You're going to need an X-ray.'

'What the hell were you doing, Evan?' a woman shouted as she stamped across to them. 'I could've killed you, you little brat.'

Vicki turned to her. 'I'm sure he's sorry. He has to go to hospital to have his arm checked.'

'Serves him right. I panicked when he crossed in front of mc.'

'You deserve a medal for the way you kept control of your car and avoided him.'

'Didn't feel like I had any control.' The woman was quietening, her stance softening. 'What if I'd hit him?'

'You didn't. That's what matters.' Vicki looked down at him. 'Cole? How's it looking?'

'Definitely broken. Mind diverting to the hospital?' It would be quicker than waiting for an ambulance.

'No problem,' she answered.

The woman was shaking her head. 'I'm Evan's teacher. I'll take him to his mother. She works just along the road,' the woman said. 'Then I'll drive them both to hospital. No argument from you, young man,' she added.

'Thanks, Mrs Waring.'

'I've got a small cotton towel in my car to use as a sling and keep that arm up.' Vicki went to get it.

Cole carefully helped Evan to his feet, and kept an arm around him when he began wobbling. 'Easy. You've had a shock.' He explained about the sling and held Even's arm away from his body when Vicki placed the towel underneath and then tied it behind his neck.

Within minutes Mrs Waring and Evan were heading up the road.

Cole turned to Vicki. 'I can't believe how lucky he was.'

She nodded. 'Doesn't bear thinking about.' Her gaze was on the disappearing car.

'We're soaked more than ever.' At least the rain wasn't cold. He was watching Vicki. Her blue eyes were clear and her mouth soft. 'Vicki?' he croaked.

Turning towards him, she looked into his eyes and smiled. 'Some things are out of our control, aren't they?'

'Sure are.' Being with her, after attending to the boy, sent a buzz of need throughout him. Hesitantly, he placed his hands on her shoulders, and when she didn't pull back he leaned forward to brush his lips across hers. Instantly, the need intensified, and he pressed closer, feeling her lips under his, her mouth opening slightly.

Oh, Vicki. He breathed deeply, drew in her familiar scent. *Vicki, my love.*

She was kissing him back, returning the pressure, drawing him in, relaxing her body into his.

Toot, toot. 'Get a room,' someone yelled out.

They jumped apart, staring at each other, their chests rising and falling fast.

'Damn.' Vicki swung around and leapt into her car.

Damn, all right. She wasn't happy. While he wanted more. Not that she'd been trying to avoid kissing him. No way. She'd been fully into it. As he had. He swore. This was all wrong. They were husband and wife, and had always had a great relationship, and now they couldn't kiss? His lungs expelled the air they were holding, and he trudged across to the car and dropped into his seat, gasping as his leg protested at the sudden movement. When he was breathing normally again, he turned to face her. 'I'm not apologising.'

Her beautiful mouth quirked, giving him some hope they'd not drag this out. 'Okay.'

He nearly laughed. But he was fresh out of laughs right now. He was hurting; in his leg and his heart. This was nothing like how they acted together. But there was the threat of their failing marriage hanging over them. 'I've never worked with you medically before.'

She turned the ignition on. 'We didn't do a lot this time.' Her voice had a quiver in it. She didn't know how to handle the situation any better than he did.

His love soared. She could tell him whatever she liked but he loved her, and that was that. Vicki existed, hadn't disappeared off the face of the earth, which had been a recurring nightmare in the dark days and nights he'd lain in a hospital bed, drugged to the eyeballs with heavy pain relief. Even when he'd stopped taking the drugs the nightmare had been a constant companion.

His apprehension over this weekend remained. Maybe he had to prove to Vicki how he felt, because she didn't believe him any more. Or believe *in* him.

She drove off, keeping a vigilant eye on traffic movement and not saying a word.

The atmosphere got more uncomfortable with every kilometre they went. Finally, he couldn't take it any more and came up with something mundane to break the silence. 'I spent last night with Nathan and Molly.'

She nodded. 'I talked to Molly yesterday. The little ones are growing fast. She sends me lots of photos.' Sadness hovered between them.

At least she'd spoken to him. Gazing at his beautiful woman, his gut clenched. The loss of their baby had taken the spark from her sapphire eyes and the ready smile he cherished. The jaunty way she held herself had been replaced with a heaviness he'd never known before, shocking him. Was she suffering from depression? She hadn't mentioned it. But then she'd told him little in their terse phone calls. It was so unlike his Vicki. Nathan or Molly hadn't said a word about her being depressed, but then they hadn't told Vicki about his injuries either. Those two knew how to keep their noses out of other people's problems and only give support when needed.

'They are little rascals, into everything,' he told her as he scoped those amazing legs that brought back some wonderful memories. Suddenly Cole smiled, despite the pain in his chest.

Her purple, low-heeled shoes matched her lilac uniform perfectly, except they were classy, not drab like the shapeless outfit covering her curves. Vicki remained a shoe-aholic. It would take a lot to change that. Something about shoes had her reaching for her bank card all too often. Their wardrobe floor had always been chock-full, with no space for a single pair of his shoes, let alone his boots and sports gear.

He heaved out a breath tinged with relief. At least one thing was still the same. There had to be others. Maybe he could let the hope in a little bit further. Or was she buying more than her normal number of shoes to fill in the gap left by the baby? By him? Probably. By signing up for the army, he understood he had let her down. Especially because he hadn't explained why he'd done it. At first there'd been no regrets. They had come later when he'd understood the price—too little time with his wife.

'Have you met the woman Conrad's started seeing?' Vicki asked, reminding him he was meant to be keeping a conversation going here.

'Not yet. Dad says he's taking it slowly.'

'He deserves some happiness.'

'True. It's been a long time on his own.' Something he might be facing if this weekend didn't go well. 'His habit of working long hours means she'll have to be patient if she hopes to spend lots of time with him.'

'I understand that.' Vicki's jaw tightened.

Ouch. He'd walked right into that one. But he understood where Vicki was coming from. What if he had tried harder to be with her whenever he'd been on base in Sydney? What if he'd talked to her more about what made him tick so she'd understand where he was coming from? Cole shuddered. That mightn't come easily, but it was something he had to get over if their relationship was to work out. She did deserve the best from him.

At least now there'd be more time for her, for them together. *If* he hadn't left it too late. When he'd told her during their last phone call that he was back in Sydney, seeing out his contract, she hadn't been full of the joy he'd hoped for. Certainly hadn't given him anything to get excited about.

Since the scandal that had affected his family he'd become cautious about letting anyone into his heart. Nathan had eventually made it as a close friend. He glanced sideways to watch Vicki manoeuvre through the traffic along the water-covered road. This wonderful woman was the real exception. From the moment he'd met her he'd lost the battle to remain uninvolved. She'd had him by the short and curlies, and a whole more. She was beautiful, funny and serious all in one, cheeky, and totally into him. Unused to being accepted so readily and completely, he'd fallen hard.

He'd skimmed over what had happened all those years ago, hadn't wanted to tell her how shamed he still felt; and how his family had paid huge consequences for him blindly trusting friends. Now he had to tell her everything, bare his faults, if he stood a chance of winning her back. Frustration burst across his lips. Why couldn't he just touch Vicki? Feel her skin on his palm? Because he wouldn't be able to stop at that. That's why. Longing ran through his veins without any brakes. Only making love would calm him.

This weekend was too important to stuff up by coming on to her when she was obviously holding back. He'd love to return home to Sydney on Sunday with Vicki at his side. Or at least with a promise that she'd follow him as soon as she finished the job at the medical centre. From what he'd heard, the GP position at a family medical centre in Rose Bay, Sydney, was nearly his. One final interview on Monday and hopefully they'd move forward—together.

Get real.

From what he'd seen so far, nothing would be that straightforward. He had a lot of apologising to do, as well as a long-overdue explanation of why he had done the things he had. He needed to tell her why he'd become the man he was, but again the hesitation stalled him. He'd lost too much already because of those so-called friends. His mum to heart failure. His father to work as he'd tried to move on from his initial, ready acceptance of his son's supposed guilt. Now he was available for Cole in a sad, less involved way, except when it came to supporting Vicki.

Cole's life compartments—before the theft, during the repercussions, and afterwards were about keeping the past away from the future. Vicki didn't belong in the past, and yet she deserved to know, if only so he could bury it once and for all. So why was he afraid to tell her? Pride, probably. An emotion that got in the way of being open and sensible. Okay, he'd add that to the list of things to discuss this weekend. In the end, it might be the easiest of the lot.

A fire engine came towards them on the other side of the road, lights flashing, the siren ripping through the air. Vicki looked sideways as it passed. 'I imagine Damon's lot will be busy pumping water from buildings.'

'You haven't heard from him?' He liked Vicki's brothers, though where he stood with either of them right now was anyone's guess. This family was very loyal to each other, almost too much sometimes, and he might find himself an outsider now. 'What about Phil?' The police would also be out in force.

'Not a word from either of them. At least Mum and Dad's house is off the ground.'

'Looks like the power hasn't been affected.'

Just then lightning cracked across the sky directly in front of them.

'Did you have to say that?' Vicki smiled easily for the first time since he'd arrived.

His heart melted all over again, which it was prone to do whenever they were together. 'Of course I did.' It used to be one of their little jokes. Vicki reckoned he always tempted fate with his wisecracks. For a brief moment he felt good.

Then she spoiled it. 'Fingers crossed you're wrong.'

Vicki had hated the dark ever since, as a teen, she'd gone to the bathroom without turning on lights and sat on the toilet, only to get bitten on the backside by a carpet snake languishing in the water. Apparently, only weeks previously her friend had nearly died from a poisonous snake bite. She always kept a night light on in the hall when she went to bed. Out at Palm Beach it would be darker than in the city if there was a power failure with no generators to keep street lights going or emergency lights glowing from high-rise buildings. She wouldn't let him hold or comfort her tonight. She was too edgy for that. Apart from the odd slip she'd been holding herself tight, keeping away from him physically and mentally since the moment he'd said hello.

'I have been known to be,' he said quietly. About a lot of things. Especially about how he hadn't been there for Vicki at the worst times. But she hadn't always given him a fair chance, either. 'Why didn't you wait until I came home to discuss how unhappy you were? It wasn't going to be for ever. Hearing you say you'd had enough over the phone was awful.'

'It would've been nicer if you were standing in front of me?' she snapped.

'No, but it might've been easier to understand with you unable to hang up on me. That's when we could've talked about everything.'

'Like all the other times, you mean? Ten minutes between parade and going to the medical unit. Or in bed after making love and you falling asleep because you'd just done seventy-two hours nonstop on an exercise. Give me a break, Cole. You never took time to actually listen to what I said.'

'I heard everything. Every time. What about me? You know it was important to me to do the years in the army.' So much for waiting until they were at the house before talking.

'Didn't know why, though.'

The car's indicator was flicking, Vicki turning onto the road that led to Palm Beach and her parents' home. Her focus was totally on the street ahead. Her hands were gripping the steering wheel and her chin pointed forward.

The need to be out of this tiny, intense space began overwhelming him. To be inches away from Vicki and not lay his hand on her thigh, or rub his shoulder against hers, was driving him insane. Not that spending the next two days and nights inside the house with only her for company was going to be much better. In this weather there'd be no getting away from each other whenever they needed to think and breathe properly and gain some equilibrium.

She turned into the driveway.

Time was up. Out of the car and into the fire.

Unless he could make her understand he'd never wanted to hurt her and that he'd do anything not to do it again—except walk away from her for ever.

Tugging the key from the ignition, she snapped, 'Come on, Cole. Losing the baby broke my heart. And you weren't there. From where I stood, it seemed you never had been when I needed you, and what guarantees did I have you would be in the future? Sure, I was sad, lonely and down. I reacted out of fear and desperation. But I've had time to think about it, and I would still do the same.'

'And you say I'm the one to let you down.'

'I'll take my share of the blame, if it makes you any happier.'

'Of course it doesn't.' He'd done wrong by her. Yes, he got that. So she had to give him a chance to make amends. And make some of her own. But he wanted to continue this conversation inside, out of this tiny, airless space.

CHAPTER FOUR

DEEP BREATH. Long sip of wine.

Say it. Ask him.

Vicki swallowed hard. She had to know before anything else. Forget that spat in the car. They'd both been venting pent-up emotions. This was her man, obviously injured. How well had he recovered? Were there long-term consequences to whatever had happened?

She carefully placed her over-full glass on the bench, her shaking hand making the liquid slop from side to side. 'Tell me why you're limping, and what else is causing you pain. Did something terrible occur while you were overseas?'

Had he been caught in enemy crossfire? That had always been on the cards, and had often kept her awake at night as she'd worried pointlessly over Cole being shot or injured whenever he was overseas with the army. But surely his CO would've informed her if that had happened?

Cole sighed, and rubbed his chin with his

palm. Returning to the table, he sank onto a chair, carefully stretching his legs out to their long length. Reaching for the bottle of beer, he rolled it back and forth between those palms that could knead her into a frenzy if she let him. Hot memories poured into her, awakening nerve endings some more.

Was that the way forward? Reconnect through lovemaking? Make the darker elements of their relationship easier to deal with? No. All that would happen was she'd give in with nothing changed. And have a wonderful time on the way. Her eyes focused on Cole's legs. Legs she loved having wound around her own as they slept. The open-neck shirt he'd changed into when ditching his wet clothes showed lightly tanned skin at the opening, making her hands itch to slip under the fabric and caress him, to feel his nipples tighten. Hers were tightening. This was hard. Impossible. He had to leave, give her some space, instead of cranking her up like a wind-up toy. Or she had to give in and tell him how much she loved him. And let go any chance of having meaning in her life that *she'd* created? 'No,' she repeated under her breath. 'No.'

He still wasn't answering her questions.

'Tell me,' she all but begged.

'An out-of-control laden vehicle ran into the light utility truck I was aboard with some of my men.' The bottle rotated back and forth faster. 'I was injured.'

'Where was this? While you were still overseas? Or after you came home?' Where had she been at the time? England? Italy? France? Or here in Cairns? 'When did it happen?'

'East Timor. Four months ago.'

He was still limping! His injuries must've been horrendous. Hang on. Four months! Around the time she'd had the miscarriage and had been trying to figure how to go on without Cole. 'You never told me. Why?'

Gripping the edge of the bench, she stared at him.

I'm his wife and I didn't know.

Opening her mouth, she let the words pour out. 'Did you think I wouldn't care? What happened to the "Together through the good and the not so good times" promise, huh? Cole?' She'd have been on the first plane out of wherever she'd been to get to his side. Forget everything else worrying her, Cole would've come first.

His mouth tightened for a moment. When he finally looked at her, those beautiful cobalt eyes were darkening with sadness. 'It's because I knew you'd come to me that I didn't tell you.'

'You didn't want me there?' Pain lanced her heart so hard it might stop any second. Cole hadn't asked her to be with him when he'd been injured. He hadn't wanted her with him as he recovered from those injuries. Here she'd been thinking she was the one who'd caused their differences.

Reaching for her glass to keep her hands busy in case she decided to throttle him, she stared at the man she'd thought she knew. Both hands gripped the stem to raise the glass. She took a big gulp, trying to drown the sense of falling into a deep quagmire of more pain and anguish. Their relationship was in a worse state than she'd imagined, had been for a lot longer than she'd realised. It was pointless to feel the slightest hope that they might find a way through their difficulties. It didn't matter that she loved Cole. Another large gulp didn't dissolve the fear starting to rise within her. They really weren't on the same page about their marriage, and it seemed they never had been.

'Vicki, no. You're wrong. Please, sit down. Hear me out.' His eyes were still locked on hers. 'Please?'

'I'm not sure I want to listen to you repeating how you didn't want me with you when you'd been injured. Obviously seriously,' she added around the thudding in her head and chest.

Her elbows hit the bench, sending sharp pain up her arms, splashing wine over her fingers. Her legs didn't feel capable of shifting her to the table where Cole indicated. Staring at him, trying to read what he wasn't telling her, she held her breath. Hear him out? Sure. She had to know the worst, get it over with. But she wished he'd hurry up while she was able to listen without being ill. Her lungs rose as she filled them with thick, humid air. 'Explain that comment.'

Another anguished sigh fell between them. 'It happened the day you miscarried. Minutes after you finished telling me and hung up.'

'What? Truly?' Cole had been involved in an accident moments after she'd dropped her bombshell on him? Was it indirectly her fault for giving him the shocking news while he'd been on duty? She'd distracted him so he hadn't seen the other vehicle until it had been too late? Though he wouldn't have answered her call if he hadn't been in a safe place. Would he? She didn't really know him as a soldier, but she did as a man who was careful and brave. Or so she'd thought. 'Were you driving?'

'No.'

She staggered to the table and slid onto the chair he pushed out with his foot. 'Go on,' she whispered. He'd been hurt, badly, if that limp and his drawn face and less muscular body were anything to go by. She was a nurse, trained to read these things. Just hadn't expected to see them knocking her husband about.

My husband.

Yes, Cole was still her husband. They weren't together, were about to discuss divorce, but in the meantime… Her heart sank. In the meantime what? She wanted to be with him.

Hold on. Don't give in now. You've come this far. See it through. Remember your mother and all she lost by giving herself over entirely to her family.

A deep breath, and then, 'I want to hear everything.'

I think.

'My driver saw the truck too late to avoid the impact. I was thrown forward, through the windscreen onto the road into the path of a car that also failed to dodge the accident. It stopped on top of me.'

She was going to throw up. Images of what a car could do to a body filled her mind. She'd seen people in emergency departments who'd been run over. Not even Cole's strong, muscular body would've been a match for wheels attached to a heavy vehicle. Deep breaths. In, out, in, out. Cole had been squashed under a truck.

'Here. Take it easy.' His large hand splayed across her back, gently pushing her forward so her head was on her knees. 'I'm fine.'

'You don't look it,' she gasped between breaths.

'Thanks for the compliment.' His light-heartedness was forced, nothing like his usual banter. But then nothing was usual about tonight. Except that kiss. Intense, filled with love—*and* fear, which wasn't usual.

Don't go there.

Slowly, she lifted her head, sat back, shrugging his hand away when really she wanted to turn into his body and hold him for ever. 'Carry on,' she muttered around the longing filling her dry mouth.

Cole placed her drink on the table before returning to his chair, this time sitting with his elbows on his knees, his hands clasped under his chin. 'My left shoulder was dislocated, four ribs fractured, three fractures to my left leg. It could've been worse. My right side was spared. I also received a moderate concussion from impacting on the tarmac when I landed head-first.'

She wanted to cry, scream, be sick, to fling herself at him. Tremors rocked her, her fingers went rigid, and her mouth fell open. 'Are you telling the truth? You are all right?'

'Yes, I am. Not perfect, but functioning okay.'

Thank goodness. Relief poured in. Cole wasn't so badly injured he couldn't get on with his life. She should've been with him throughout his surgeries and rehab. He hadn't asked for her. The disbelief was still ringing in her head. 'You didn't ask for me.'

'No. I stalled the CO when he was determined to let you know what had happened and make arrangements for you to fly to Darwin to meet the plane I was medevaced out on.'

'I'm down as your next of kin.' The details were there in black and white on his contract. 'Did he call your father instead?'

Cole shook his head. 'No. I explained about the miscarriage and said I wanted to be the one to tell you about the accident when I had been operated on and my concussion was gone.'

'Obviously, he agreed.'

'Eventually. Mainly because I refused to have surgery until he did.'

'You were that determined.' It wasn't a question. 'Thanks a lot, Cole. It shows where we were even back then.' She tried to stand, had to get away from him, but her legs had other ideas, dumping her back on the chair, so instead she reached for her glass, took a small sip, and waited for the pounding in her chest to subside enough not to feel like a jackhammer was at work.

Cole tipped his head back and drained his bottle. Then he looked at her again. 'You're wrong. I knew you were unhappy, and that there were things I'd screwed up, but I've always believed our marriage was in reasonable shape.'

'Right,' she snapped around the bitterness

tainting her mouth. Last time he'd come home she'd told him how she felt she was waiting in the wings instead of putting a life together with him. It was also when she'd become pregnant. 'You always expected me to be happy while I worked and waited for your short visits home.'

'I was wrong. I know that.' He watched her with such intensity it worried her. What was he about to say?

She remained silent, her fingers tapping the table top.

'There was nothing I wanted more than to have you with me. But...' He stopped.

Tap, tap, went her fingernails.

Finally, 'I injured my spine. At first the doctors weren't sure I'd walk again. You'd said we were over. I did not want you rushing to my side because you felt you had to take care of me.'

She stared at him, totally confused by his comment. And hurt beyond belief. Anger rose, unstoppable. She couldn't do this. Toughen up. She had to. Had to hear him out even if he never listened to her. Then she could go ahead with getting on with her life. But first she'd listen to the rest of his story, and try not to give in to the horror of his injuries and fall into his arms. Because that was really what she wanted to do the most. 'Go on.'

He went to the fridge, got another beer and

brought the wine bottle over to top up her half-empty glass, though there was more on the table than had gone down her throat. 'Even as I was flying through the windscreen I held onto my phone so tight the indents on my fingers were there the next day. I would not lose my only contact with you.' He held up a hand as she went to protest. 'No, I don't remember your number off by heart. At least, I didn't then. I do now.'

Too damned late.

She said nothing. What could she say that wasn't full of anger and hurt and disappointment? And worry for Cole. Yet he'd had his phone all through whatever had happened after the accident and still hadn't called her.

'Vicki, I was desperate to talk to you, to hear your voice, to make sure you were coping, and get some comfort myself, but how could I expect anything when I hadn't been there when you were miscarrying our baby? The pain and grief in your voice tore me apart. How could I think I deserved you to come to my side after that? After the other times I'd neglected you? I won't use the excuse that I had no choice once I signed up with the army any more. I made that decision in the first place, so I manned up and took responsibility for letting you down, starting with not begging you to come to me when I was unable to go to you.'

'Which is it, Cole? You felt guilty? Or you were afraid I'd come out of a sense of duty, not love?'

'Both.'

She stared at this man who'd never once told her he could be selfish, never admitted he might've done the wrong thing by them when he'd signed up for the military. His answer was direct, and honest, and still filled with that stubborn pride so typical of him. Now what? Forgive and forget? The ball of anger and pain that had been with her for months was loosening, letting go a few of the strands that kept it wound tight. Could she let him off that quickly? That simply? Without explaining that she had a future of her own she wasn't prepared to put aside to follow him wherever he chose to go. No, she still had a battle on her hands, but at least the hope had returned to flicker behind her ribs. 'Were you admitted to a hospital in East Timor?'

'Only to have my spleen removed by an American army surgeon, before being flown down to Darwin for orthopaedic surgeries the following day. It was a little like flying in ICU, the number of wires and tubes attached to me.'

She closed her mind on that picture. 'Multiple surgeries?'

'Yes.'

'After a splenectomy.' This only got worse

every time he opened his mouth. The pain he must've suffered being transferred before those fractures had been dealt with. Vicki shuddered. 'Cole, you should've told me. I would've been there as fast as possible, no matter what had gone down between us earlier. I'd have wanted to be with you, despite everything, not because I felt I had to.'

He nodded.

'You told Conrad everything?'

He blanched. 'Yes.'

Forget the fluttering hope. The flutter turned to lead. 'Did he race to be with you?' Honesty could be a bit much to swallow sometimes.

'He came to see me in Darwin.' His chest rose. 'I made him promise not to say a word to you. He argued with me, and I'm sure he picked up the phone to call you more than once, but eventually I won.'

'I bet he kept up to date with your progress.' This hurt so much. She was his wife. She loved him. 'You didn't even mention anything during those few awkward calls we had.' She might understand his restraint, but didn't accept it. 'That was wrong.' What he'd done made her angry, sad, and very frightened. 'I can't forgive this in a hurry.' If ever.

'Vicki, sweetheart, I'm being straight with you, not hiding anything this time. I am sorry

I've hurt you. I will make it up to you, if you'll let me.'

Loud knocking on the front door interrupted her. Which was probably for the best. Who knew what would spill out of her mouth at the moment? She was hurting so much it blinded all common sense. Once spoken, words could never be taken back. Though right now she couldn't think of anything she'd want to withdraw once uttered. Had she ever really known Cole? As in really, honestly, truly?

'Vicki, you there?' someone called out.

She leapt to her feet. 'Helen?' Thank goodness for intrusions. She could put her whirling mind on hold, unless Helen only wanted a cup of sugar.

The neighbour from three houses down stood at the door she'd opened, water pooling at her feet. 'You're needed. Bill's fallen off his ladder onto the drive. He's unconscious.'

Hearing what the woman said to Vicki, Cole leapt to his feet, ignoring the pain in his leg, glad of a diversion. Seeing the emotions roiling in Vicki's eyes had decimated his already broken heart. What had started out as trying to do the right thing by her had turned into the biggest mistake of his life, and it had kept growing until now he had no idea if he'd ever be forgiven and allowed the chance to rectify things in their marriage.

'Cole, you hear that?' Vicki called out. 'Cole's a doctor,' she told the woman standing on the porch.

At least Vicki wasn't denying he had a role to play in what was obviously an emergency, despite her anger at him. Anger he'd expected, and deserved. Telling her the truth only made resolving their differences all the harder, but honesty had to be a part of sorting this mess out. If they ever did. Telling her about his injuries and how he hadn't called for her had been excruciating. Not least because he'd finally seen how wrong he'd been, how deeply he'd hurt her. That meant nothing was going to be as straightforward as he'd thought. Explain, apologise, and get on, that had been his hope. Not the reality, he saw now. Talk about being an idiot. Did he deserve her love when he could do this to her?

'Cole?'

He shook his mind clear of their problems. He was right behind her. 'Has anyone called an ambulance?'

Helen looked directly at him. 'Yes, but all emergency services are very busy. They'll get someone here as soon as the next ambulance is free.'

'That figures. I'll get the pack.' Vicki headed for her father's medical storeroom.

Cole was with her as she tapped in the security number to unlock the cupboard. 'Let me look at the drugs we might need.'

'All yours. Want the defib?'

'Might be wise. I'll carry it.' Thankfully, she didn't argue. It took only a moment to find what he might need, covering the basics for pain, shock, cardiac arrest. After hauling on a jacket and shoes, he rushed up the road with the women.

Vicki asked Helen, 'What was Bill doing up a ladder in this weather? He's at least seventy-five and not as stable as he used to be,' she added, for his benefit.

'Then some of his bones have likely broken on impact.' But it was the head injury worrying Cole most at the moment. The man was apparently unconscious. That wasn't good.

'His guttering was blocked with leaves and flooding the internal garage,' Helen replied. 'Stubborn old coot didn't think to ask anyone for help.'

'Where is he now?' Cole asked.

Helen glanced at him, quickly looked away. 'I know you're not supposed to move someone in this situation but he was soaked and with this weather we all thought it best to get him under shelter so we rolled him onto a blanket and slid him across the floor to the back of the garage where there's a modicum of shelter.'

There was no changing that so as they raced up the driveway, Cole said, 'You're right about getting him out of the rain.' Fingers crossed. Someone holding a large sun umbrella over the man might've been a better option, but these people were obviously not medically trained and couldn't be blamed for trying to do their best to helping a friend.

Gingerly lowering onto his knees beside the elderly man, Cole immediately began listening to his airway, and finally nodded. 'Breathing's shallow, but his chest's rising and falling regularly,' he told Vicki as she knelt on the opposite side of Bill.

'Bill? It's Vicki Halliday—Vicki Chandler. Can you hear me?'

The old man didn't move.

Vicki continued. 'Cole's here too. He's a doctor.'

No response.

She reached for Bill's wrist to take his pulse.

'Bill,' Cole said. 'We're going to check you all over. I don't want you trying to move at all. Okay?' He'd continue talking to him while finishing his primary survey in case the words got through. 'Pulse?' he asked Vicki.

'Low. He's sweating profusely.' She was placing patches from the defibrillator on Bill's now exposed chest so they could get a reading of his heart. Immediately, the rapid heart rate was apparent.

'Shock and probable internal blood loss.' Feeling Bill's abdomen, groin, listening to his chest, Cole found swelling, signs of haemorrhaging. 'The liver's taken a knock.'

'His arm was caught in the ladder and we had trouble removing it,' a man told him. 'It was jammed between his upper body and elbow.'

Why had they moved the man? Cole stared at the arm now lying beside Bill's body. More damage might've been done. His gentle prodding told him the elbow was shattered. He left the limb as it was, not wanting to inflict further injury. 'Right, now the head.' Gently touching the skull, he quickly found trauma that explained Bill's unconscious state. 'We need an ambulance fast.' He looked around at the people standing back, watching him and Vicki attend to their neighbour. 'Can someone call 000 and give me the phone when you've got the service on line?'

'On it,' a woman answered.

'There a neck brace in that pack?' Cole asked Vicki.

She gave him a quick glance before returning to watching the defib screen. 'Yes.'

'I'll find it.' Helen opened the bag and began removing containers of bandages. 'This what you want?'

'Thanks.'

The other woman handed him the phone. 'I've explained that we've already called this in so he knows where you are.'

He nodded and spoke to the dispatcher. 'I'm a doctor and I understand there're delays getting an ambulance but we have a GCS of two. Severe head wound, major fractures of ankle, knee and elbow, also internal bleeding.'

'I've contacted the rescue helicopter service. They're about to lift off. Can you put someone on so I can explain what we need done for the chopper to land safely?'

'Sure. And thanks.' Cole looked around. 'I need someone to take this. We need the road cleared for a helicopter.'

A man grabbed the phone and Cole returned his attention to Bill.

'BP's slowly dropping,' Vicki informed him. Calmly, she rechecked all the readings and noted them down on a pad, which Helen had found in the pack, to go with Bill to hospital. Nurse Vicki was in play. Not the woman whose heart he had broken. Or who was breaking his. Even in nurse mode she was gorgeous.

His own heart squeezed. Damn, he loved her. He had to win her back. Had to.

'Have to get this collar on,' she reminded him, dragging his thoughts back to where they needed to be.

'Let's do it.' With practised ease they quickly had the collar in place. Even though Bill hadn't moved at all since they'd arrived, a sudden jerk could cause serious damage to his spine if there was any trauma.

Cole continued examining his patient, now checking the less urgent injuries. Blood stained the trousers around the knee area. There was a tear in the fabric that he used to rip down the leg to expose the damage. The bleeding was minor, the least of their worries. The right ankle was at an odd angle. Again, there was nothing he could do until the paramedics got here with splints and a stretcher.

It seemed for ever before the thumping of rotors suddenly slammed their eardrums from directly above the house. The rain had hidden the approach of the flying machine now hurling water in all directions outside as it descended to the road beyond the end of the driveway where many locals had come out with torches and lanterns to light up the area and stop any traffic that might come along.

Within moments paramedics were kneeling

beside Bill, and Cole filled them in with his observations before stepping away, glad there were others to lift the stretcher. His leg was throbbing. The emergency crew was in charge now, and had all the gear needed to transfer Bill safely to hospital. There was nothing more he or Vicki could do. Time to head back to the house and that unfinished conversation.

Except what else could he tell her?

That he'd missed her more than ever while lying on his back for weeks on end, waiting for his bones to heal enough to be able to get up on crutches and start walking again. How the fear brought on by her words, which had kept ringing in his head throughout the sleepless nights, hadn't let up. Even when he'd been concentrating hard on walking and ignoring the pain of those broken bones, he'd kept hearing her desperation.

I can't do this any more.

As long as he lived he would hear the sadness, the anguish in her voice on that day. His darling Vicki believed he had let her down.

He had.

She'd been gutted over losing their baby. Her distress had vibrated through the ether to him. She'd needed him with her, not helping strangers. She'd needed him to talk about their loss. How *had* she got through those days and weeks afterwards? By talking to Julie? Her parents? Molly and Nathan? Hopefully, she'd had someone's support, otherwise there was still a lot of pain to be worked through. Not that it would've disappeared anyway, merely eased a little. He knew, because he held his own knot of pain deep inside. It would've been better for both of them if he hadn't been in another country at the time.

Never again. From now on he'd always be there for her.

If only she would give him a second chance to show how much he meant it. How much he loved her.

CHAPTER FIVE

'I HOPE BILL makes it.' Vicki strode out alongside Cole as they headed back to her parents' house, aware that he didn't move as freely as he used to, despite saying he was fine.

He limped, ran, limped, ran. 'I can't lie. That head injury is a worry,' he agreed.

Quite likely Cole was still in pain from those fractures, especially when trying to run, as the impact when his foot hit the pavement would be sharper than when he was walking. She slowed a little, trying not to be obvious, ignoring the rain. There were plenty of dry clothes in the house. 'I can't believe he climbed a ladder in this weather.' Vicki let out a long, regretful breath. 'Actually, that's not true. He's a stubborn old man by all accounts, and apparently since his wife died last year he often says there's no reason to keep himself safe any more.'

'That's sad.'

'Terribly.' This was getting too glum, and

for now she wanted to take a break from being down and angry and hurt. Nudging Cole in the arm, she said quietly, 'He had a good team on his side.' She held her hand up in the high five gesture, and felt happy when Cole's hand touched hers. Warm and strong. Lifting her spirits, reminding her not everything had gone bad in her life. Here she was, with Cole, tending to someone in trouble. Nursing satisfied a lot of her need to help others. Caring for Bill alongside Cole had been even better. They'd understood what each should do without hesitation. As they used to with most things.

'Not bad at all considering we've never worked together before today.' His smile was slow and filled with tenderness. The smile that had always made her feel special.

And, surprisingly, it still did. Butterflies beat behind her ribs. They might make this work. If they could get through the next two days without too many disagreements. 'First time for everything.' She returned his smile, not quite sure if she was referring to working together or something deeper.

Turning onto the path leading to the house, she said, 'Just because we've been along the road don't think you're getting out of cooking the steak.'

'I wouldn't dare. Anyway, I'm not letting you near it. I like mine rare.'

'You still not letting me forget the first meal I ever cooked for you?' It had been a disaster. She'd been so nervous, not wanting anything to go wrong, so of course the steak had been overcooked. Not to mention the onions and mushrooms. Inedible would be a kind description.

'Hell, no. I've had a lot of mileage out of that night.'

'True.' Unlocking the front door, she turned to him gleefully. 'Of course there were the daffodils you sent me at work.'

He held his hands up. 'Okay, we're even.'

She headed for the kitchen and a bottle of water. 'Plastic flowers last a lot longer than the real thing, but don't quite have the scent or happiness about them.' He'd ordered them online while he'd been away, thinking he was in touch with a Sydney florist, when it had been a Chinese warehouse and the box had taken ten days to arrive.

'You couldn't have kept real flowers to rub my face in for all this time, though. Still got them?' he asked, then stopped.

She admitted, 'Yes, I have.' She didn't want to get into talk about having packed up all her possessions from their apartment and bringing them with her to Cairns, leaving his gear and some photos behind. For the moment they were getting along and she'd like to keep it that way for a while longer.

'I didn't keep the steak.'

'Benji enjoyed it.'

Another touchy subject. He hadn't been around when she'd had to make the decision to put the dog down. Of course Cole couldn't have changed the outcome of the accident that had put Benji under the vet's care, but sharing the anguish of telling the woman to do the right thing quickly and painlessly might've been some comfort. The day she'd collected Benji's ashes she'd broken down, cried for hours, missing Cole so much her heart had ached for days.

They'd scattered the ashes together the next time he'd been in Sydney, sneaking out to their pet's favourite park at night so as not to get caught. Holding hands as they'd said goodbye had been some consolation, though the anguish of making the decision about Benji on her own had haunted her for some time.

She still missed the mutt. Might be time to get another one as part of moving forward. Her stomach tightened. Suddenly, she felt overwhelmed with a need to make the most of being together, to remember how easy it could be between them. Lately all she'd thought about was how they didn't get on any more.

'I'm getting out of these wet clothes and bringing the lanterns into the kitchen in case we do have a power outage.'

'I'll put the drugs back in the cabinet before I change. Want me to top up the bag as well?'

'Definitely. Not that we used much out of it.'

'Water or beer?' Vicki asked Cole when he returned later.

'Water.' He paused in front of the TV she'd turned on. 'The road's flooded north of here.'

'Nothing unusual in that. It happens every time there's a rainstorm. The council's geared up for it, but it does mean Port Douglas is cut off. The internal road to Cook Town is closed too.' She handed over a bottle of icy water as she watched the extent of the flooding being shown on the screen. 'They're saying the rainfall is heavier than usual for a monsoon. Bill might've been lucky the helicopter got here.'

Cole shook his head. 'No, even the smaller machines can fly through quite a lot. The deluge out there wouldn't stop them, only lack of visibility might have been an issue, but they did fine.'

'You'd have seen a lot of that overseas.'

'I did. Flew in a few too. Large suckers.' A pensive look came over his face. 'The last flight was when I was flown to the local hospital. Didn't see a lot on that one.'

'Were you conscious by then?'

'Yes, though not totally *au fait* with what was happening. The medic had filled me with enough painkiller to drop a horse. Or so it felt. I wasn't used to being pumped full of morphine.'

'Bet you are now.' She tipped water down her throat, and wiped her mouth on the back of her hand. If only she'd known. *Yes, Cole, you owed me that much.* 'You still get pain in that leg.'

'It's a bit shorter than it used to be. The fractures have healed but there're residual aches and pains, especially when I overdo things. It'll eventually quieten down. Or so I've told patients in the past. Guess I'll find out how correct my notes from training days really were.' Cole's tight smile went straight to her heart.

He'd have been determined to get back up and running in as short a time as possible once he'd known his legs would work. Damn it. He could've been a paraplegic. Yes, and she'd still have loved him. Straightening her shoulders, she refused to let his smile or his near miss with paralysis knock aside her resolve to fight for what was important to her, and thereby to them both.

'You want a salad with that or shall we have steak sandwiches? I bought some fresh buns today. There's chilli jam in the pantry,' she added, no longer in the mood for making a salad or cooking vegetables. Sleepless nights tossing and turning while thinking about Cole and this weekend were catching up.

'You've got me. Buns and jam it is. I'll turn on the barbecue. I'm starving.'

'It's getting late, for sure.' Where had the time gone? The landline rang. 'I hope that's not another accident.' Vicki picked up the phone. 'Hello?'

'Hi, darling. We've been watching the news and wondering if everything's all right at the house.'

'Hi, Dad. No problems here.' She hurried to put his concerns to rest. 'Lots of water, but no flooding around Palm Beach.'

'That's good. How's everything else? Cole make it?'

'Yes, just in time as the airport closed not long after.' She needed to divert her father before he came up with questions she had no answers for. 'We got called to help Bill. He'd gone up his ladder to clean the guttering and fell off. Did himself a lot of damage and had to be flown to hospital. He was lucky in that respect as the ambulances are in high demand right now, and it's taking them time to get anywhere.'

'That's not good. I hope he's going to be all right.'

'He was unconscious, has a few fractures.'

Again she changed the subject. 'You still in Broome?'

'Yes, moving south tomorrow. I hope you gave Cole the key to the drugs cabinet.'

'Of course I did.' Why wouldn't she? 'It's handy having everything here. There might be more calls before this is over. The rain's not expected to ease till tomorrow at least.'

'Can you put him on?'

'Dad,' she warned, alarms bells ringing in her head. Her family loved her and would do anything to keep her happy, including interfering with her marriage if they believed they had the answers to solve her problems.

'I'm not going to tell him how to behave or to be careful what he says to my daughter. You're big enough and tough enough to do that yourself. This is about the medications in that cabinet.'

Relief sank in. Her dad was always ready to stick up for her, and while it was great to have her family at her back, she really did not want any interference this weekend. 'Thanks. Please mean that. I've got this.'

'You know what you want more than any of us, my girl. Just sort it sooner than later, all right?'

'I'm doing my best.'

'Vicki,' Dad growled lightly. 'I've learned my

lesson after seeing how your mother held herself back for all of us, especially me. I don't want the same for you.'

'Aw, Dad,' she gulped. 'I need that.' His backing made everything a little easier to deal with. 'Here's Cole.' She passed the phone to her husband. Yes, whatever came about, he still *was* her husband. 'Dad wants a word.'

Immediately, wariness clouded Cole's face.

She put him out of his misery. 'It's okay. Nothing personal.'

'Marty, how's things?' Cole strolled out to the barbecue, which was sheltered by a plastic roof.

The lights flickered, went out, came back on. Vicki moved to the bench where the lanterns stood in case it happened again. Being left in the dark was the last thing she wanted.

Cole was back, phone still to his ear. 'Okay?' he mouthed, hand on her shoulder.

She nodded, glad of his company, trying to ignore the warmth his touch brought.

He smiled again. 'Good.' He'd know she wasn't being entirely honest, but it was part of the routine to say she was fine. 'Hang on, Marty, I'll go down to your office and check that.'

Vicki watched him walking out of the room, the limp not as noticeable in his long stride at the moment. Still as sexy as ever. Her heart lurched.

Oh, Cole. I've missed you more than I'd have believed possible.

What would he do if she followed him, wrapped her arms around his waist and laid her cheek against his chest? Or stretched up and kissed him again, showed him how much she still loved him? Made love with him?

You think?

The conversation still to come loomed between them, would taint any lovemaking.

She needed a distraction. Fast. After checking the matchbox was full, she went to get a torch from the cupboard, trying to calm her racing heart. The dark was her enemy. Snakes could slither through the house and she'd be none the wiser unless they bit her on the way past.

Cole dropped the phone back on its stand. 'Didn't know anyone still used landlines.'

'It's Mum. She's prefers it to these modern new-fangled things.'

'That's Anna to a T.' He smiled—almost as though he knew how hard it was for her to pretend his smiles meant nothing any more. 'I'm glad you didn't get that gene.'

'As if.' She was right up to date with phones and apps, which made setting up her business simpler. With the help of a computer whizz she'd started playing with website designs. As she planned to continue nursing while hiring out staff to hospitals and medical centres, accessing files and messages anywhere was important and required a streamlined system easily used under pressure. A flicker of excitement warmed her. Her own nursing agency. The doctors at the centre where she worked at the moment had been very encouraging when she'd run the idea past them. There was a lot to do before she was ready to start seeking out placements and staff, but she'd get there.

'Those buns ready?' Cole called from the deck, where he stood under cover, cooking the steak.

'Nearly.' Letting out a frustrated sigh, she tried to shake away the thought that Cole was going to fight her on this one. He had to be told, regardless of the weekend's outcome. If, by some remote chance, they made up and decided to give their relationship another go, her agency would be an important factor. What worried her was her expectancy he'd say they'd be living in Sydney, not Cairns. An agency would work there too, yet the city was vast with a large population and she didn't think she wanted to try to set up there. She'd have more competition, or she'd have to limit the area she covered. Which could work, she conceded.

'Earth to Vicki. Rolls?'

* * *

Cole took the steaks inside and got two fresh water bottles from the fridge, handed Vicki one. 'You all right?' She'd been miles away when he'd popped his head around the door to check if everything was ready.

'Sure.' She pushed a plate with a buttered roll in his direction. 'Hungry as.'

There'd never been anything wrong with her appetite. It was one of the things he'd liked when they'd first met. None of that nonsense about only eating small portions and ignoring the foods she really enjoyed. But then they'd connected on so many levels right from the get-go. 'Me, too. The dry sandwich and bland coffee on the plane did nothing for my appetite.'

Exhaustion shaped her smile. 'You should've helped yourself to something when we first got home.'

His appetite had quietened down as he dealt with being with Vicki, treading carefully so as not to upset her any further. 'It's all good. I'm enjoying this.' He thought back to the night they'd first met. He'd been intrigued to find out who Nathan had thought might be his perfect match, and had gone along to the party fully expecting to have a laugh and maybe a good night with no follow-up and, wham, bam. Literally eyes meeting across the room.

When he'd first spotted Vicki he hadn't realised she was his date. His gut had told him nothing was ever going to be the same, while his head had mentioned he had to find Nathan to say, 'Forget who you've jacked me up with. I've found my match all by myself.' Instead he'd found himself owing his mate for bringing Vicki to the party to meet him. They certainly had *connected* that night, and never looked back.

Until recently. Not that he was glancing backwards, more like trying to figure out what was ahead. That kiss had rocked him to his feet. Kisses were part of them, as was lovemaking. Being stuck in this holding pattern turned the importance of enjoying each other upside down. They needed to talk, fully and frankly.

Yet it was difficult to start. Like where? What came first? At the moment they were awkwardly comfortable with each other, as though pretending the past few months hadn't happened. But they had, and they itched just below the surface. Explaining his failure to get her to fly to him after the accident had been difficult, but it was done. Maybe not quite finished, or accepted, but it was on the table.

He'd believed he'd been doing the right thing at the time, and hadn't wanted to add to her pain, or his. He'd learned to make quick decisions about difficult situations in the hope he didn't hurt anyone again. Had he been too quick?

Vicki said he was wrong to have decided for her. Hadn't she left him without so much as talking through the miscarriage and other problems first? Sure, she'd been hurting, but he'd deserved a chance to go over what bothered them both, too. 'How are you coping with the miscarriage?'

She put her fork down, and looked at him. 'The loss is huge still. I have times when the tears flow, my heart breaks, and I want to scream at the world. But that happens less often now. I'm getting there, I guess.'

'It's never a quick fix.'

'And you? How do you manage?'

'I had lots of time to think about it while lying on my back. Yes, the pain left me feeling raw, and wishing we had been together to face what had happened. I think I'm over the worst. Not that the sense of loss will ever go away entirely.'

'I agree.' She nodded slowly. 'It has been the hardest thing I've dealt with. I struggle talking about it still.'

'Might be best if we did.' When she didn't answer, he added, 'Whenever you're ready, I'll be here.'

I love you, Vicki. Please don't ever forget that. Don't think I've stopped. I haven't. Won't.

The steak refused to go down his throat. He

chewed some more. What if he'd truly lost her? For ever? No. It couldn't happen. Could it? That blinding recognition of his feelings when he'd seen her racing to get out of the rain at the medical centre had told him more than anything else could how much she meant to him, and how nothing had changed. That short kiss had ramped up the stakes. Except now he was aware how quickly problems could escalate and would work hard to prevent them becoming a nightmare.

Vicki glanced up and locked wary, sad eyes on him. 'Thanks.'

He'd never seen her so unhappy. And he was the cause of most of it.

'Tell me again you're going to be all right, that those injuries are healing properly,' she said quietly.

He reached across the table for her hand and squeezed gently, felt the jolt that rocked her. 'Seriously, I'm going to be fine. Already am. Might not climb Everest any time soon, but there's nothing I can't do that I didn't used to be able to.'

Vicki returned the pressure on his hand before withdrawing. 'It must've been terrifying.'

That gentle squeeze softened the ache in his heart. 'It happened so fast I didn't have time to think.'

Start being yourself. Be the guy you were be-

fore the theft ruined everything. The one who shared everything about himself, not just a select few issues that are easy to resolve.

It had been so long he doubted he even knew that version of himself, might not be that guy any longer. 'Holding onto my phone was the only thought running through my head.' Sigh. 'And the thought that it was going to hurt when I landed.'

'So you were aware of what was happening all the way through?'

'Until I hit the road. I didn't see the vehicle as it ran onto me. It hurt. A lot. Mostly later.'

Vicki was blinking hard and fast. 'Thank goodness for small mercies. That'd be a picture most likely to stay with you for ever.'

His throat thickened. 'I remember being relieved when I came round and saw the medics beside me. It meant I was alive.'

'Now I understand your reaction when I braked too hard.'

'Instinctive, I suppose.'

'It seems weird that after all the time you served on active duty overseas you got injured in a traffic accident.' Those eyes were still blinking. 'Though you wouldn't have been there if not for the army, so I suppose it does make sense.'

Don't cry on me. Or for me. I don't deserve your tears.

His throat was closing. 'Them's the breaks.'

As she ate, she seemed to withdraw. Then, 'So where do you stand with the army now?'

'I'm on paid medical leave for another month while receiving ongoing treatment, then I'm taking early discharge due to my injuries. There was another contract on the table but I never intended to continue as a career soldier. I wanted to come home. I'm a doctor and would like a full-time career as a general practitioner. A real job.'

'The army wasn't real?' Vicki snapped.

He huffed a low sigh. 'One where I'm fixing people, not driving around in armoured vehicles looking for trouble, and then picking up the pieces when we find it.' Serving his country was one thing, but soldiering had never been him. Sure, he'd been a good officer, had looked out for his men, but he'd done what he'd set out to do and kept his promise. Now he wanted to get back to his real passion—medicine. And Vicki.

'Don't regret what you did or it becomes worthless.' There was an accusation in Vicki's voice that stabbed hard, like a sharp knife under the ribs.

'I do have regrets, and they're all about you, me, us. But I can't change a thing. All I can do is go forward.'

'You want a hot drink?' When he nodded she

got up to put the kettle on. 'That's true for both of us.'

What was she saying? That she didn't want to go back to being with him? Or, if she did, it was going to be different this time? Or that she had things to tell him he wasn't expecting that might blow his socks off? Here he'd been tentatively thinking the evening was progressing in a good way, and now the doubts were back. The edginess in Vicki's stance, in his thoughts, was tightening with every moment. 'Vicki?'

Sliding her hands into the pockets of her shorts she stared at the spot between her bare feet. 'I would've come to you, you know?'

'Yeah, I do.' Hadn't they dealt with this earlier? 'Whereas I couldn't fly over to you. I would've if it had been at all possible.'

The kettle switched off but Vicki didn't move. 'Which is one reason why you didn't believe you could ask me to join you. Not only the spinal injury. Do you know how that makes me feel, Cole?'

'Hurt.'

'Try angry. Try let down. Try disappointed. And hurt, sure. You were injured the same day I had the miscarriage. I would've joined you. No question.' She hesitated, drew a breath. 'It feels as though you were paying me back for something I have no idea about.'

It was his turn to be hurt. 'You're wrong,' he growled. 'I believed I was doing the right thing.'

Those sad blue eyes locked on him. 'By me? Or by yourself?'

'You said you'd had enough, our marriage was over. Would you have thanked me for guilting you back into it?'

Her eyes widened. 'Guilt wouldn't have had anything to do with it. Instead we could've talked face to face, fixed the problems pulling us apart, not made them worse.'

'Isn't that why I'm here now?' The divorce couldn't happen, not until they'd covered everything lying between them.

'It's too late.'

His heart plummeted to his toes. 'Why?'

'You've never really heard anything I've said about what I might want. Even now you can't accept I would've rushed to you, for you and us.'

He was not going to be forgiven in a hurry. If at all. His gut crunched hard. This wasn't going well. Not that he'd expected to be wrapped in another hug and kissed wildly, but just a little understanding would go a long way right now. He'd have sworn Vicki never held grudges. Seemed he'd got that wrong too. Or had she learnt to because of him? He could do with some levity before he sank too low. 'Can I ask you something?' Since when did he have to check before saying whatever was on his mind?

'That depends.'

'Can I have tea? Not coffee.' When her mouth started to flatten again he hurried to carry on. 'I'm not taking any of this lightly. It's hard, and I want to cheer you up. Though I guess that's expecting too much.' Not once in the years he'd spent with Vicki had he felt so useless, unable to say what he wanted without looking for implications he didn't mean.

With quiet efficiency, Vicki made two mugs of tea. 'Here, get that into you, though we'll probably end up sweating something awful in this humidity.' She sat down opposite him again and picked up the TV remote.

Obviously the conversation was over—for now. 'Thanks.' For the tea and backing off the hard stuff for a while. It didn't mean the problems had gone away, they were only on hold. Then the urge to pick up Vicki and kiss her long and hard, to make love tore through him. Flapping his hand in front of his face, he muttered, 'It's damned hot.' Every inch of his body was heated, pounding with need.

'That's Northern Queensland for you. I'm used to it and yet it still gets to me.' The news channel came up on the screen.

Could he get used to it? Move here if that's what Vicki wanted?

They watched in silence for a little while, then he said, 'Nothing's really changed from earlier. That has to be a good sign.'

'Or we're in the eye of the storm.'

Like their marriage. 'You're a box of cheer, aren't you?' he groaned, finally at ease again, though still a little tight in the groin. The need to kiss her wasn't backing off.

She yawned, and checked her phone. 'Blimey, where did the evening go? It's after midnight. I should go to bed, though I doubt I'll sleep.'

So much for kissing. She wasn't inviting him to join her.

'Might give it a try myself. It's been a long day.'

If only they were going to share a bed, he could deal with the ache that had taken over his body. But he'd been shown to the third bedroom without a hint of remorse on Vicki's part when they'd first got here. It was the first time they'd been in the same building and not slept together since the night they'd met.

His gut tightened in on itself. Talk about bringing home how far down the wrong track they'd gone. Would there be any turning around, getting back together? Behind his ribs, his heart slowed to a sad rhythm. Did Vicki see this weekend as their final time together? Was she going to tell him she didn't love him any more? That the divorce was a foregone conclusion?

'Or we could sit up all night and thrash out what's bugging us,' he said quietly, suddenly desperate to move on. Get this done one way or the other. No. He would not give up. He loved Vicki. There was only one conceivable outcome.

Vicki's head flipped up, her eyes wide and startled. 'No,' she gasped.

'Why not?' At least they could start the ball rolling so he knew what he was up against. He waited. And waited as she fidgeted with the hem of her shirt, looking everywhere but at him.

Finally, she raised her head and locked her gaze firmly on him. 'You're right.' She stopped, the heat in her eyes fading. 'Oh, Cole. This is crazy. Who'd have thought we'd come to this? I can't believe it.'

'It doesn't have to be all bad. We need to discuss everything that's worrying you. That's why I'm here.'

'Don't you have concerns about how we've blown it?'

'I understand you've got issues with the time I've spent away from you, and because I didn't ask you to come to me when I was in hospital.' He sipped his tea, staring over the rim of the mug at the woman he loved so much. 'I'm here to listen, to work with you to get our marriage back on track.'

'It's not that straightforward, Cole. There're two of us in this mess.' She fiddled with her fingernail, picking at it with her other hand. 'Why did you really join the military? You always avoided the question. I might've understood and coped better if you'd told me.'

The doorbell rang loud and sharp, cutting through the air like a laser.

Vicki scrambled to her feet, muttering, 'Go away. Can't you see we're busy?'

'Who's that at this hour? Have we got another accident to respond to?' This time he definitely did not want an interruption to their evening. Leaping off his chair, Cole followed her down the hall where a large shape loomed behind the thick glass panel in the front door. 'Careful,' he warned. 'Could be anyone.'

'It's safe around here.' Despite her words there was tension in Vicki's shoulders as she pulled the door wide. Then her shoulders returned to their normal position. 'Hello, Merv. What's up?'

The fireman at the door was saying, 'Hi, Vicki. There's been a hill slide that's taken out an occupied house. We need you and a doctor ready and waiting when the family's rescued. Damon says your ex is here. Is that right?'

Her ex! Cole's blooded heated in an instant. Not bloody likely.

I'm still her husband, thank you very much.

He stepped up beside Vicki who'd turned to him.

'Yes, Cole is here.' Even though they hadn't touched, she must've felt his anger because she laid a hand on his arm. 'Sounds like we're needed again,' she said quietly, as though trying to ignore her own annoyance with the man before them.

If only Vicki felt the same about him. She was the only person he wanted to need him.

He nodded abruptly. 'I'll get the emergency kit. Do you know what we'll be dealing with?' He stared at the man, trying not to dislike him for his blunder.

'I was only told to pick you up if you were available.'

Well, he was, despite his anger. Being a doctor came before most things. Just not before Vicki, and she was going with him so he'd settle down and do what was required of him. And then get back to that conversation they'd begun.

CHAPTER SIX

'COLE'S FURIOUS,' Vicki acknowledged as Merv drove them towards the hills on the opposite side of the main road north.

So am I. For being interrupted at a crucial moment and for that 'ex' comment.

They hadn't made that a definite. Had Damon really called Cole her ex? Or was this man reading too much into whatever her brother had said about there being a doctor at his parents' home?

'Is Damon at the scene?' she asked the fireman. Because if he was, he was going to get an earful. He should not be talking about her private life to anyone.

'He was when I left. The guys are focused on stabilising the house to protect the family caught inside. Others, including neighbours, were trying to reroute the slip as small amounts are still coming down directly behind the property but it's not really feasible in these conditions, especially without a bulldozer and digger.'

'What state's the house in?' Cole asked from the back seat of the large four-wheel-drive vehicle. He sounded as though he'd got his anger under control, though Vicki knew he'd still be gritting his teeth.

'The back's stoved in. That's where the bedrooms are—were. The front rooms look normal, except for a dangerous lean, and the ceiling's down in places. When I left to collect you no one had been inside to check it out. It's too dangerous until we get joists in place.'

'Anyone been calling out?'

'A woman, presumably the owner, was heard yelling to get her children out,' Merv told them.

Worry rolled through Vicki. Children in a disaster area. They'd be terrified, and so darned vulnerable.

'I hope the kids don't try anything silly to get free.' Damon's bollocking was on hold.

'Two neighbours are talking to the children, though not getting any responses. They figure if they keep chatting it might help keep everyone calm.'

'If it's at all possible I'll be going into the back section as soon as we get there.' Cole wasn't questioning Merv, he was telling him. Officer mode in operation.

She smiled to herself, before announcing in

a similar tone. 'So will I.' It didn't come out as strong and determined as she'd intended.

Naturally, Cole was onto her immediately. 'You wait outside and I'll bring those children out to you when possible. The firemen will help me.'

'The hell with that. I'll be needed there almost as much as you,' she snapped.

'Vicki, I don't want you in any danger.'

'Back at you.' Cole was not getting injured again. For one: he wasn't as fit as he used to be so recovery would be harder. For two: she loved him, and did not want anything bad happening to him. For three: ditto. She sighed. There was no doubt about her love for this man she'd always known to be her other half. Walking away would be nigh on impossible. Not that she wanted to.

What? Wasn't that what this weekend was supposed to be about? Not from the moment he'd said hello outside the medical centre it hadn't. She straightened up in the seat. So she had to explain her plans carefully so he'd understand what she hoped to accomplish, or their love would eventually crumple into a bitter heap.

'Settle, you two. No one's going in that building until Damon gives the okay,' Merv said. 'As for you, Vicki, I doubt you'll getting anywhere near those flattened rooms. We all know Damon won't let you get within range of any danger.'

True. Why did it have to be her brother's crew working this job? 'We'll see about that,' she grumped.

Cole tapped her on the shoulder. 'In, out, girlfriend.'

Unexpected laughter bubbled over her lips. He'd came up with it the first time he'd ever seen her lose her temper. Tenderness stole through her. This was what she'd missed. The small expressions of love they shared, as much as the big ones. A light touch was as important as hot sex. A look, a kiss on his jaw, his fingers massaging between her shoulder blades. Communications that belonged only to them. A personal language all their own.

Why am I doing this? Holding out on Cole when he's my other, stronger half is crazy. And necessary.

The doubts backed off slowly, to a point they lingered in the back of her head, not foremost for once. They hadn't talked enough yet and the first night was well on the way to morning. The next few hours were going to be taken up with other people's problems. Even if miraculously no one was injured, they'd still need checking over and given lots of reassurance that they were safe.

'Here we go. Hold on.' Merv dropped a gear

and began driving slowly but purposefully into the torrent of water racing down the road in front of them. 'That flood marker shows the depth hasn't changed in the time I picked you up so we should be good.' Just then the ute lurched sideways and he deftly swung the steering wheel left, then right, then straight ahead.

Vicki gripped the edge of the seat and stared out the side window at the swirling brown water lit up by the headlights. Merv knew what he was doing. There was nothing to get stressed about, but this wasn't something she'd done before. 'Lots of logs and debris in there.'

'Also mud from the landslides further up, though no other house has bought it that we know of.'

'That's good news,' Cole said. 'What's the scenario with the rescue service? Are the helicopters still flying?'

'They were last time I asked, but if anyone needs hospitalisation we'll have to get them across this first. Can't have a chopper anywhere near the hill. The pounding from the rotors could bring down more land and trees onto other houses near the one we're going to.' Merv hadn't let up on the accelerator even when Vicki knew she would have. He was keeping the speed consistent, driving correctly for the situation.

'You're good at this.'

'Had plenty of practice over the years in the service.' Then the ute was climbing out of the torrent onto *terra firma*. 'Right, nearly there.'

Within minutes they pulled up beside the fire truck and bundled out into the rain. Cole retrieved the emergency pack, wincing as he slung it over his shoulder.

Vicki studied him for a moment. He hadn't mentioned an injury to his back or shoulder, but then a vehicle had parked on him so it stood to reason he had some muscular problems, and then there was that initial spinal issue. Again fear engulfed her for what might've happened to him. His injuries were bad enough, but what if they'd been worse? She might never have got the chance to talk to him again, might've had to live always knowing her last words to him had been terrible. 'Sorry,' she whispered.

He glanced down at her. 'Later, okay?'

Nodding, she slipped her hand in his, drawing on his strength as she walked alongside him to find out what was happening regarding those poor people in the house ahead of them. Or what was left of it. Nearing the hillside, she gasped, 'That's unreal.' The back of the house looked as though it had been built into the hill and then covered with soil until it could no longer be seen. 'How can anyone survive that?'

'Yeah,' Cole sighed, his fingers tightening

around hers before he pulled away. 'You've got to wonder. Especially the kids.'

'Cole, Vicki, there you are.' Her brother crossed to them. 'So far we know there are three boys, aged six to ten, and their mother in the rooms at the back under that debris. We've talked to the mother and one of the kids, but nothing from the other two youngsters.'

One child talking was an improvement on what Merv had told them. But she wasn't relaxing yet.

'Can I get in there?' Cole asked.

Vicki restrained herself from snapping that she was going with him. She'd just do it. Best to listen to everything Damon had to tell them first.

'Yes, we've shored up some of the rafters and made a way in. Once you're inside there is a spacious cavern that used to be the bedroom on the far side. It didn't collapse as much as the others. Two men are in there, assessing the situation and trying to reach the two non-responsive children. They'll get you to the boys as soon as it's possible.'

This could turn out to be a dreadful situation. Vicki drew a deep breath. It was always hard dealing with seriously injured people, or worse, but kids knocked her sideways every time. They had to get to them fast, do everything within their power to save them. 'Let's go.'

Cole didn't even argue. Not a word. Just said to Damon, 'Lead on. We need to get in there.'

Her brother looked from Cole to her as though he was about to tell her to stay outside.

'Damon, Jack has heard a kid crying,' one of the firemen called.

Damon sighed. 'Come on, you two. Let's go save this family.' He started towards a group of rescue workers, then paused. 'By the way, the woman, Karen, is heavily pregnant, and complaining of pain.' He turned away and continued to the house.

Cole grimaced. 'It just keeps getting better and better.'

'Fingers crossed the pain is from shock or a hard landing when the house was knocked out around her and not labour,' Vicki said. 'No baby needs to be born in these circumstances.'

'Is it my imagination or did the rain just get heavier?' Cole glared up at the darkness above them.

'I doubt it could get heavier. I mean, how much water can clouds hold?'

'Thought you'd be used to this, having grown up around here.'

'I am, but doesn't make it any nicer to deal

with. And I've been in Sydney for a few years so I'm out of practice.'

'A good reason to return there.' Cole nudged her gently.

The weather was the least of her concerns. 'We'll see.' They'd reached the side of the entombed house and she shivered. It was going to be just as wet inside. And dark. She'd try not to think about that. The fire truck had a pair of large searchlights focused on the house, but how much of that light was getting into the interior was an unknown at the moment.

'You can still stay out here,' Cole said quietly. 'I'm sure one of the neighbours would be happy if we used their home to see to any of these people when we bring them out.'

Then she wouldn't have to deal with the dark. Wouldn't be looking over her shoulder for snakes, even when it was unlikely there'd be any here considering the number of people tromping all over the place and banging at posts and house walls. In, out. 'I'm going with you.'

'Getting more stubborn by the minute.' His smile hit her hard, and deep.

And ramped up the sense she should just cave and hug him, hold on for ever. 'Better believe it. Let's get started. Those kids will be terrified.' She headed for Damon, who was waiting for them at the edge of the gaping hole they were going into. 'Lead on, brother.'

'It's going to be cramped in there.'

Cramped would've been comfortable. The bedroom they found themselves in mightn't have been completely crushed but the internal wall had been forced sideways and loomed over them, forcing everyone to hunch down to move around. How Cole managed, she had no idea.

'It's safe for now,' one of the men tried to re-assure her.

'Let's do this fast as possible.' Cole nodded.

On the floor sat a woman looking shocked and scared. Her nightgown was torn at the shoulders and her neck and arms were smeared with mud. Blood stained her forehead and the side of her head above an ear. Someone had wrapped a blanket around her, but she was still shivering.

Vicki ignored the creepy feeling she was getting from the room where little light was making its way through from that fire truck. A large torch helped somewhat, but she couldn't stop herself from looking around for snakes.

Cole laid a hand on her arm, said quietly, 'All clear.'

He knew her failings too well. 'Thanks.' Then she crossed to the desperate woman and knelt down. 'Karen? I'm Vicki, a nurse. This is Cole. He's a doctor.'

'My kids. Where are they? Have they got them out?' Karen cried, snatching Vicki's hand and holding on hard. 'Where are they?'

'The men are working on getting them out safely. They've been talking to them.' Not saying only one had responded. That wouldn't help this distressed woman one little bit. 'Can you tell us if you're in any pain?'

'Leave me, go to the children. I can wait.'

Awkwardly, Cole hunched down beside them. 'Karen, I hear you but until the children can be moved out of their room we can't do anything for them. We can't get in there, and if we tried we'd be getting in the way of the men trying to make it safe for them. For now I'd like to check you over and see to any injuries you might have.'

'No, leave me, go to them. Now. Please,' she begged. 'Talk to them if you can't reach them.'

'As soon as I'm told I can get in there I will. I promise,' Cole told her. 'In the meantime, let's make sure you're all right so that when your kids are out you can hold them.'

Vicki held her breath. She totally understood this woman's need for her children to be dealt with first, but Cole had a point. Why waste time waiting for the children when Karen might be in need of help?

Finally, Karen nodded. 'All right.'

'How far along is your pregnancy?' Cole asked.

'Thirty-six weeks.'

Damn. After the trauma of having her house knocked from under her and her children stuck in their rooms, Karen was possibly in labour. 'Have you been having contractions?'

'I think so. Sometimes my belly tightens, and there's a pain like labour, only not so strong as I've had with my others.'

'How far apart?'

'I don't know. Not often.'

'Let's leave that until the next one,' Cole said. 'I want to check that wound on your head. Do you remember being hit?'

'Not really. It all happened so fast. There was a loud bang, lots of noise and then the wall was coming towards me and the bed slamming across the room.'

'Do you think you might've lost consciousness?' Cole asked as he gently probed the wound with a gloved finger.

'I don't know. Everything's a blur.' Karen blinked and tears slid down her cheeks. 'Except it's real.'

Vicki held her hand tighter. 'Everyone's doing whatever they can to get you all out. Are you hurting anywhere else?' The creaking and groaning of timber was scary.

'I didn't even realise I'd hurt my head until this man said he was going to look at it.'

'That's shock. I'm going to check your pulse and then we'll have a look at your body to see if there are any other injuries.'

'Cole.' Damon was crouched behind them. 'Can you come with me?'

Vicki's heart sank at the quietness in her brother's normally robust voice. One of those kids was in trouble. Had to be. Glancing at Damon, he was giving nothing away in front of Karen.

'Need me?'

'Stay with Karen.'

She felt certain this wasn't about her hang-ups over being in the dark but about looking out for this frantic mother. Nodding, she said, 'No problem.'

Karen wasn't stupid. 'Have you got through to the boys? How are they? Is one hurt? All of them?' With each question her voice rose.

Damon drew a breath, tightened his shoulders. 'Karen, we've got through to the bedroom. The boys are talking so that's a good sign. Cole will take a look and help us get them out.'

'Thank you.'

They were all talking, or still only one? Vicki wasn't asking in front of their mother.

Cole stood up as much as he could. 'I'll let you know as soon as I've seen them.'

'Vicki, you must go too. I don't need you. My boys are more important.' Then she burst into tears. 'I wish their father was here.'

'Where is he?' Vicki asked.

'Arlo works in the mines in West Australia. Six weeks on, six off. He should be here, not over there where he's no use to us at all.' Karen stared around what used to be the bedroom she shared with her husband when he was home. 'I know he's doing it for our benefit, and that we are well set up because of the long hours he's worked, but he's missed out on so much with the kids. And me.'

Another man who wasn't around when he was most needed by his family. Vicki couldn't help glancing at Cole, and gasped. The stunned look on his face told her he'd been thinking much the same.

Dragging her eyes away, she took Karen's hand again. 'You're being very brave. Your children need you to keep focusing on that. Okay?'

Hypocrite. She'd been a wimp, screaming at Cole that he should be with her and not running around playing soldiers. But she'd meant it, had been hurting, had wanted no one but Cole with her at the time. Just as Karen wanted her husband here, and not on the other side of the country.

'Go to my boys, please. I want them to have all the help they can get.'

She nodded. 'I understand.'

'It's going to be darker in there,' Cole said softly. 'And a lot more crowded.'

'I'll deal with it.' She wasn't about to let Karen down. The boys needed her to step in for their mum.

'Agh…!'

Vicki spun around, whacked her head on the leaning wall, and swore under her breath. 'Karen?'

The woman was panting, gripping her stomach. 'A contraction. More like the real thing this time.'

'I'll stay with you. In fact, let's get you out of here.'

'No. Leave me. Go to the boys. It's been a while since the last pain. There's still a way to go. I hope.'

Spoken like a woman who'd already had three babies. 'If you're sure?' When Karen nodded, she added, 'Yell if you need me.' Then she followed Cole on hands and knees through to the remains of the boys' bedroom, and tried to ignore his sexy derriere. Like that was possible, even in the crazy situation they found themselves.

* * *

Cole's stomach dropped as he took in the sight before him. How could anyone—especially three little boys—survive the disaster that had only hours ago been a normal room? The walls resembled a mix of wood chips and wooden spears. The ceiling beams had crashed to the floor, one flattening a bed in its way. Under that beam lay the distorted body of a young boy. His eyes were wide open, filled with fear. His hands were clenched together over his chest. At least he was alive.

Where were the other two lads? Were they in a better or worse state? Karen had a point. The boys' father should be here, and yet he understood the man's reasons for being away. Which was more important? Giving his family a good start financially, or always being around, handing out love and joining in when things were to be celebrated or fixed? It gave him more to think about concerning him and Vicki. Not that he'd joined the army to get a better life. Far from it.

Vicki bumped into his butt, reminding him why he was there, and that he needed to forget about anything but saving these lads. He said to the boy lying in front of him, 'Hello. My name's Cole. I've come to help you. What's your name?'

No reply.

Cole waved his hand in front of the boy's face

and got a blink in return. So he was aware, but too shocked to speak. 'I'm a doctor, and this is Vicki. She's a nurse.'

Nothing.

'Hello, young man. I'm going to hold your hand.' Vicki had moved up and now took one cold, tiny hand in hers and carefully laid a finger on the pulse in his wrist. 'You're a very brave boy, being so quiet.'

Blink.

Cole reached for the boy's legs and began carefully running his hands along the areas not held down by that beam. Judging by the odd angles, there'd be fractures below the knees. Looking over his shoulder at Damon, he said quietly, 'I'm going to administer morphine before your men attempt to lift that beam.' Checking for bleeding, he sighed with relief when he found none. Digging in the pack, he removed the drug and a needle, saw the fear grow in the boy's eyes. 'It's all right. Your legs are sore, so I'm going to make them feel better. That's good, isn't it?'

No reply.

Vicki took the vial he held out and read the date out before handing it back. Then she leaned closer to their patient. 'Okay, young man, how old are you?' When no answer was forthcom-

ing, she continued, 'I think you must be seven.'
Silence. 'Or are you eight?'

Blink.

'Ah—told you. Eight. Now, what's your name?
What's a cool boy's name…?' She scratched her
chin and stared at the floor. 'I'm thinking…
Jack.'

A slight shake of his head.

Vicki pushed the sleeve of the boy's shirt up
to expose his arm for the injection. 'Mickey.'

She was good. But then Cole knew that. He
tapped the boy's vein.

Another shake of the small head. 'Callum.'

Bingo. She'd done it.

'Callum, eh? That's a great name for a brave
boy.'

Cole slid the needle in and pressed down on
the syringe.

'Ow!' Callum cried.

'Sorry, mate. But I've finished.' Cole pulled
the needle clear. 'Vicki's right. You're very
brave. Can you tell me where you hurt?'

'My legs don't move.'

'That's because there's a hunk of wood on
them. The firemen are going to shift it away
very soon and then we'll be able to take you out
and have a good look at you. Okay?'

Callum nodded, then bit his lip, tears threatening.

'What's up?' Vicki asked. 'You hurting?'

'Where's Mum? She hasn't come to see if we're all right.'

'That's because she can't get through here with her baby tummy. It won't fit through the gap in the wall. She's all right, okay? You'll be able to see her soon.'

'I want her now.'

Cole's heart clenched for this brave wee man. 'You'll see her when the firemen carry you out of here. That all right?'

'I suppose.' Callum yawned as the drug took effect.

Cole glanced over his shoulder. 'Not long now,' he told Damon.

'The men are ready.'

Cole nodded. He wanted to ask Callum if he'd heard anything from either of his brothers, but that might add to the lad's distress so he turned back to Damon, said quietly, 'Where are the others?'

'Beside the wardrobe that looks like something out of a demolition site.'

Vicki crawled toward where Damon indicated, glancing left and right and sucking in a breath at the shadows darkening the corners. Nothing slithering and dangerous. She didn't relax.

Cole thought of the day he'd taken her to a

snake sanctuary with the brainless idea that if she got to touch one, maybe hold it with a zoo keeper watching over things, she'd get past her paranoia, but that'd earned him a blasting and hadn't solved her problem. Once they returned to Sydney—he wasn't thinking if—there was less likelihood of her coming across her least favourite creature compared to up here in Queensland.

Two burly firemen squeezed into the small space. 'Hey, Callum. We're going to get this board off you and take you somewhere dry. Okay?'

The boy nodded. 'Is it going to hurt?'

Cole took his wee hand in his large one. 'You can't feel your legs now, can you?'

'No.'

'Then you won't notice the board moving away. I'll keep holding your hand, okay?' The little fingers were gripping his tight.

With a lot of straining the roofing beam was lifted enough for Damon and Cole to pull Callum free; they slid him onto the stretcher ready on the other side of the narrow opening.

Cole asked, 'Are there any leg splints in the fire truck emergency gear?'

'Yes. Want them now or when we're out?'

'Out. Callum's not feeling anything at the moment and it's best to move him somewhere safer.' It felt like an age since he and Vicki had arrived, but a glance at his watch showed it had only been ten minutes. One almost safe, two to go. 'We'll stop by Karen on the way and get her to agree to going outside with us. She's more help to her lads if she's out and safe.' His mind went to Vicki. He didn't want her in here either. Especially if that hill came down some more. But trying to talk her out of being with the lads was a waste of time they didn't have to spare. He called to her, 'I'll be back in a moment. You all right in there?' Not that she'd tell him, however afraid she was.

'Sure. Got more fractures here.'

Great. 'I'll hurry.' He had to make sure Callum didn't have any other, more serious injuries he might've missed in the semi-dark.

'No worries.'

He'd always worry when Vicki was in danger. No one had actually said that more of the hillside could come down on them. There was no need. With the torrential rain still persisting it was a given that anything was possible, so they had to work fast, yet carefully, to extricate this family. And get Vicki the hell away from here.

No matter where they were in their relationship, nothing mattered more to him than keeping her safe. Nothing. Not even this family he was helping.

Sorry, guys, but that's how it is. I love her and will do anything for her.

Hopefully, that meant getting back on side and staying there for ever.

CHAPTER SEVEN

VICKI KNEW THE moment Cole returned, and not only because he blocked the light reaching her and the two boys, as well as the fireman who'd stayed in here from the moment the lads had been found. It was the way her skin tightened and her fear of darkness backed off. He'd always made her feel safe, no matter what the circumstances. 'They're taking Callum to hospital?'

'Merv's boating him across to the other side now. A neighbour's with Callum, making sure he's not moving around, and will go through to the hospital as well. An ambulance has got through and is waiting on the main road.'

'Hope they get another ambulance here ASAP.' She nodded at the boy sprawled on the floor in front of her. 'This is Lucas. He's unconscious, head trauma, BP low, swelling in the abdomen, irregular breathing. And this other little guy is Toby. He's as brave as his brother, Callum.' She smiled at the wee fellow. 'He's got a headache and a bloody nose, but no other injuries that I can find.'

'Hi, Toby. Where does your head hurt?' Cole asked as he did a visual appraisal of the boy.

'There.' Toby touched his forehead carefully.

'He fell out of bed onto his face when the wall crashed into the room. I can't find any trauma on his skull. His speech is clear and distinct.'

'Good. Hold out your arms for me, Toby,' Cole instructed gently. 'That's it. Nothing sore?' When Toby shook his head, Cole said, 'Stretch your legs in front. They look fine.'

'He's got off lightly. Want me to take him out while you attend to Lucas? I'll be back in a minute. Hopefully with another stretcher.'

'Do that.' Cole was already working on the prone boy, listening to his breathing while fingering his skull and on down his body, looking for more injuries. Fast yet careful, he wouldn't miss a thing. This was a side of Cole she hadn't got to see in action, yet she wasn't surprised at how he dealt with urgent trauma.

Lifting Toby to his feet, she took his hand. 'Come on. Let's get you out of here. Watch your head on those boards.' She had to crawl along behind him to avoid banging her skull. Talking nonstop kept her moving, and Toby not looking around at the disaster surrounding them. She was relieved to see Karen had left, probably under protest, though she might've been willing to accompany Callum and try to make him relax more.

'Sis, who've you got?'

'Toby. No serious injuries, though best he goes to hospital for a thorough check-up. His case isn't urgent; he can wait for his other brother.'

'What's happening in there?'

'Cole needs another ambulance fast. A helicopter would be even better. Also a stretcher. Or a plank if there isn't one,' she improvised. 'Lucas is in a bad way.'

Damon nodded. 'I figured. I've talked to Search and Rescue and they're doing their damnedest to get transport here for the boys. The helicopters were temporarily grounded but they're about to fly again. Apparently, the rain's eased somewhat, though it's impossible to believe that from where we're standing.'

'Right, where do we put Toby while waiting for transportation? I need to get back to Cole and Lucas.'

'His mother's in that house down the drive. It's safe there, far enough away from any further slips, and not likely to be flooded. You take him down while I find something to carry Lucas out on.'

'Right.' It wasn't totally dark. She could manage. If she didn't think about slithering bodies on the ground. 'Lift Toby onto my back, will you? It'll be easier that way than if I have to keep looking out for obstacles for both of us.'

'Sure. And take this. I've got another.' Damon handed her a torch before swinging the boy onto her back. 'There you go, young man.'

As she started down the sodden track towards the house her brother stopped her.

'Stay down there, Vicki. I'll go in and help Cole with the last boy.'

She shook her head. 'I'll be back.' She wasn't going far from Cole for any longer than necessary.

'No, you won't. In the last few minutes there's been a couple of minor slips and we're acting on the side of caution. I don't want anyone else going into that wreck of a house who isn't absolutely essential to saving Lucas, and those in there are coming out fast, no matter what state the boy's in.'

The urgency in his voice made Vicki's stomach crunch tight. 'Why are you standing here talking to me then? Get in there now. Warn Cole, the others. No, I don't want you going in there either. It's dangerous.'

He wasn't listening to her, already facing the entrance the men had created.

She stood in the rain, her feet glued in the mud, her heart pounding and her breathing shallow. Hell, her body had been getting an internal workout since Cole had arrived. He and Damon were in danger. So were Toby's brother and one of the fire crew.

Please be safe. Please. Please. Please.

They couldn't have got this far with rescuing the family to have it go wrong now.

Please.

The sound of rocks rolling downhill broke into her pleas, sharpening her fear.

Someone scanned the hill side with a spotlight. 'Another small slip. That whole hill could go any minute.'

'What? *No.*'

'Hey, Vicki, that you? Get down to the house now. The boy needs to be out of the rain and safe. So do you.' Merv had returned.

'I'm not going anywhere until I see everyone come out of there.'

'Yes, you are. Think of your patient and what being out in this is doing to him. I'll make sure Cole joins you as soon as they're clear. We'll need to bring the third boy down there anyway. Now go.'

The thudding behind her ribs increased as she trudged through the water and mud, desperate not to slip, and turning every few steps to see if anyone had made it out yet. She wouldn't look at the hill, didn't want to see it come hurtling down on top of the ruin the previous slip had created. This time it would be on top of those she loved.

Banging on the open door of the house, Vicki called out, 'Hello. I've got Toby here. Is Karen about?' How was the woman managing with contractions and one son on the way to hospital and the other two hopefully following him soon?

'Come in. You must be the nurse. I'm Ester.' A middle-aged woman appeared before her. 'Here, let me take Toby. Hello, my darling, how are you?' She sent Vicki a questioning look.

'He's fine, though we need him to go to hospital for a full check-up.'

'Toby,' Karen shrieked from the doorway. 'My boy, come here.' She scooped her son out of Ester's arms and hugged him tight, tears streaming down her face. 'Thank you, Vicki. I'm so glad you and Cole made it here. Who knows how we'd have managed without you.'

'Everyone's been working their butts off to save your family but, Karen, I have to warn you that Lucas has more serious injuries. Damon is working on getting him out of here and into hospital as soon as it's feasible. Cole also wants Toby to go with him, just to make sure he's as good as we think.'

Karen's knees sagged, then she drew a breath and straightened again. 'Can I go, too?'

'That will depend on the transport that can

be arranged.' Vicki ached for this brave mother. 'We'll get you there ASAP, I promise.' She changed the subject. 'How are those contractions coming along?' Fingers crossed they'd backed off.

'Picking up the pace.'

So her fingers were no use at all. 'It might be an idea if I examine you.'

'Soon. I want to hold Toby for a while.'

Heavy footsteps sounded at the front door, then Damon's voice called out, 'Hello, Ester. We're bringing Lucas inside.'

'Don't try and take your boots off. The carpet's a mess already.' Ester rushed to make room in the lounge for the makeshift stretcher Cole and Damon were carrying in.

Cole looked around, his face tense until his eyes lighted on Vicki. 'Hey,' was all he said, but the simple word held a wealth of care.

He loved her. Nothing had changed there. She'd known that all along, even when she'd been trying to justify leaving and heading away while she came to terms with her life and what she'd do next. 'Hey, yourself.'

His face softened, and his lips turned up into a smile all for her.

She gave him one back, love warming her throughout. 'How's Lucas?'

The smile slipped.

That bad, huh? Her smile faded too. 'Damon, any luck with the helicopter?'

'It's coming, but will have to land on the other side of the flood waters, especially now there're more slips occurring. The houses further along have been evacuated but if we can avoid them being bowled over then we will. Merv's going to take the boys across one at a time in a motorised dinghy.'

'I'll go with them if they don't send a doctor,' Cole announced to the room in general.

Vicki saw Karen stiffen.

'I want to go,' the boys' mother cried out.

'There won't be room for anyone else in the chopper,' Damon told her briskly. 'I'm sorry. It's more important for a doctor to accompany the boys.'

'We've asked for the ambulance to come for you, Karen,' Cole said. 'But it could be some time off. There's a high demand for more urgent cases at the moment. Vicki will stay with you in the meantime. And me, if I'm not required to go in the chopper.'

Again tears steaked down Karen's face. 'I tried phoning Arlo but got no answer. I need him. The boys need him.'

'Keep trying,' Cole said. But it wasn't Karen he was looking at. It was Vicki.

She felt it a punch in her chest. Longing

soared. Likewise relief. Cole understood Karen's despair because he'd heard it all before. But did he really understand? Properly? Fully? Did he get that unless things changed and he discussed future plans with her, made sure they were on the same page, wanted similar things, they weren't going anywhere together? She deflated like a balloon stabbed with a pin. So far they hadn't achieved much when it came to resolving their differences, and it looked like they wouldn't be getting home where they could talk together any time soon. There was a badly injured boy in the room, not to mention a baby on its way. 'Karen's definitely in labour.'

Surprisingly, Cole grinned. 'Why wouldn't she be? It's the way the night's going.'

Karen grimaced at him. 'All very well for you to be cheerful.'

'I'm not really,' Cole said apologetically. 'But I'm grateful you're all out of that building and the boys will be taken care of in hospital. Is there someone you can call to be with them until you get there?'

'My in-laws. They won't hesitate. I'll phone them.' Then Karen's face scrunched up with pain, and she clasped her stomach with the hand that wasn't holding onto Toby.

Vicki was with her instantly. 'Breathe. That's it. You're doing well. Hey, Toby, do you want to give Ester a hug?' Thankfully, the little boy reached across to Ester's open arms, giving his mother room to move.

'Tell me when it stops. I'm going to time the next contraction.'

'They're about seven minutes apart,' Karen gasped. 'I don't believe this. Where the hell are you, Arlo?' She stared at Vicki. 'Okay, it's going away.'

Glancing at her phone, Vicki noted the time. 'Think I should examine you now.'

'Hang on.' Karen held her phone to her ear. 'Arlo, call me as soon as you hear this. We've got problems. Big ones. The house has gone. The boys are going to hospital. And the baby's coming. We need you. Love you.'

Vicki sucked in a breath, and glanced at Cole. She hadn't ended her call to him that night of the miscarriage with an 'I love you'. No, she'd said she'd had enough, couldn't do it any more. Her gut churned. How soon could they get away from here? More than anything else she wanted to talk with Cole, explain her feelings and find out more about his own needs, find a way out of this together.

An array of emotions crossed his face as he watched her. Sadness, sorrow, disbelief all mixed up there. Similar sentiments to those slamming around her skull.

Guilt battled with her sadness. She hadn't uttered those three special words to him once since that night. Not when he'd been listening, anyway. She'd been afraid he'd see right through her attempt to stand up for herself. Though often in the middle of the night, when she couldn't sleep and her pillow was drenched with tears, she'd cried out how much she loved him.

In the beginning Cole had regularly told her he loved her, but as the months had passed he'd said it less often, until finally he'd stopped altogether.

Why hadn't she kept her mouth shut and held those terrible words inside? Or at least stopped long enough to think about what Cole had to be feeling about the miscarriage? Right from then they should've talked about it. It would've been easier without these past months hanging between them when she'd disappeared to the other side of the world, and he'd been fighting to get back on his feet while still occasionally talking to her as though she hadn't done something so horrible to him.

Yes, she had been selfish, and it had taken Karen's reaction to her husband not being there when she needed him so desperately to see that. Did that mean she'd go back to Cole without talking about their futures? Did it? No. She couldn't do that either.

'Are we going to get some time to ourselves?'

He nodded. 'Yes. Definitely.' He turned to focus on Lucas, though there was little to be done. A fully equipped operating room was required. In the meantime, Cole would do everything possible to keep the boy stable while they waited for the rescue flying machine to arrive.

'What are the chances of a doctor being on board the chopper?' she asked. Usually there would be, but who knew tonight when the rescue service was in high demand?

Cole answered without looking up. 'I told Damon one was necessary and Headquarters confirmed they'd send someone from the rescue centre. Otherwise I'll go with him and one of the paramedics might have to walk home.'

'That'll make you popular.' Disappointment flared. So far everything had worked against them.

'I figure, but too bad. This wee man comes before egos. Though, seriously, if they have to they'll probably squeeze all of us on board and it will be me walking back here. Not the other way round.'

'You could stay with my in-laws,' Karen said from the other side of the room.

No, he couldn't. He had to get back somehow. Vicki swallowed the expanding disappointment, and gave in to the urge to be *with* him. She was tied in knots of desire, and it was getting close to impossible to ignore them with each passing hour. Not that sex had been on the agenda this weekend. Not unless they suddenly made everything go away and were happy. They'd worked well together with all the injured people they'd been with, which went to show they were still in sync on some things, but it wasn't anywhere near enough. They'd be in sync in bed, for sure. The heat in her veins dissipated, replaced with sadness.

Cole was telling Karen, 'I'm here to spend time with my wife so I'll find a way back to Palm Beach no matter what.'

Her heart melted. Maybe giving in and following him wherever he chose to go next, get a job and have all the spare time available to spend with him—if he was around and not off on some medical project or working every hour available in a hospital or clinic—was the right thing to do.

Looking at him, she couldn't help but smile. He was gorgeous. The almost five years they'd been together hadn't changed her feelings. That physical attraction that had had her falling into bed with him the very first time they'd met still hummed in her veins. That instant rapport and understanding of each other still lit up her mind, and other parts of her body. Combine everything and no wonder she'd fallen head over heels in an instant and not once had come up for air—until the miscarriage.

She had lost a lot of time with Cole so he could follow his career choices, and mostly she'd coped by working long hours and surrounding herself with friends, not acknowledging that unsettling feeling she was missing out on so much. Until the last year when too much had gone so wrong and her world had rolled over. Julie had even asked if she was depressed, but she was certain she wasn't. Now Cole was here, and so far refused to let her walk away without a fight. Typical Cole. And one of the qualities she admired about him, she reminded herself.

'Cole?' she called quietly. 'We'll get time to ourselves, I promise.'

He grinned his special just-for-her grin. 'As long as nature backs off and gives us a break.'

'We'll hide up in the folks' house and ignore any more knocking or phone calls.'

'As if either of us would do that.'

'True,' she sighed. 'Let's hope—'

'Ahh…' Karen groaned, cutting through their moment. 'That hurts. Like a knife in my belly.'

Vicki nodded. Interruptions were the way of things tonight. 'I wouldn't know what that felt like.' Her smile dipped. She would if she hadn't lost the baby. Don't go there. Not now. There was enough drama going on without thinking about her own problems. 'Your contractions are now at six minutes. Long way to go yet.'

'Thanks for nothing.' Karen grimaced. 'Cole, how's Lucas?'

'No change. Which is better than him getting worse.'

'I can't complain about you not giving it to me straight,' Karen muttered. 'So what's taking so long with that helicopter?'

'There's a bit of a storm going on out there.' Cole leaned over Lucas and listened to his breathing. Hopefully, his mother didn't notice the unease creeping into Cole's demeanour.

Damon walked into the room. 'Right, we need to get Lucas and Toby across to the other side now. The chopper's minutes away. Cole, we want you to go with them in the boat. Merv will take you and both boys. It'll be a tight fit but the pilot doesn't want to stay on the ground any longer than he has to. Vicki, you okay holding the fort here?'

'We'll manage. Cole? If you end up going to Cairns Hospital with the boys, don't do anything risky to get back.'

Get back quickly, so I know you're all right, but don't put yourself in danger.

'We'll see that he gets a lift with one of the

crews if necessary. Is Lucas ready?' Damon asked her man.

'Yes.' Cole stood up and crossed to Vicki. 'I'll be back as soon as possible.' His mouth brushed a light kiss on her cheek. 'Look after yourself.'

'You, too.' Her knees softened, and she stepped closer, felt his warmth and strength. Oh, Cole. 'Hurry back.' Be safe and sensible, *and* hurry back. She kissed him back, longer and deeper. Now who needed to be sensible?

Relief soared when Cole gingerly stepped out of the dinghy on the other side of the flood waters and heard a woman in dark blue overalls say to him, 'You Cole Halliday? I'm Bridget Ford, emergency doctor for the rescue services. I understand we've got a stat two patient?'

He'd get to spend the rest of the night with Vicki. 'I'm Cole. The seriously injured patient is ten-year-old Lucas. He was unconscious when the crew got to him, and there's been no change in the time I've spent with him. Suspected internal bleeding in the abdominal area. Fractured leg, and possibly ribs. Trauma to the skull.' Relief was still running through him. For Lucas and the medical help he desperately needed, and for himself because he wasn't flying to the hospital. Vicki's softening towards him had started a flutter in his chest that hadn't abated throughout the short ride in the boat watching over Lucas.

'Right, load and go,' Bridget said. 'We've got a stretcher ready at the back of the chopper. Bringing it to the boat meant getting it soaked and the boy already has enough to deal with.'

Cole held up a hand. 'There's also a second boy, Lucas's brother, Toby. He checks out fine, but I want him to go to hospital anyway.'

'We'll find room,' Bridget agreed.

Cole slung Toby onto his back and reached for one end of the makeshift stretcher in the boat. 'Ready, Merv?'

'Yes. On a count of three.'

Within moments Lucas was at the back of the rescue chopper and being swiftly but carefully transferred, and Cole waited until Bridget was ready to take Toby. Then he stepped back, letting the rescue medics take over and do their job. 'Good luck,' he called. Now he could return to Vicki. He'd be sharing her with a woman in labour desperate to get to her sons, but at least he'd be with her. His steps were jaunty as he turned back to the boat.

'Cole?' Bridget called. 'I've got a message for someone I think is with your lot. Karen?'

'Yes.' He nodded. 'The boys' mother. She's in labour.'

'Then you'd better pass this on.'

He listened carefully, nodded, and felt the familiar guilt kick in. 'That's great news.' News that Vicki would've wanted to hear the night she'd miscarried.

'You notice the rain's down to a drizzle?' Merv asked as they climbed back into the boat. He revved the motor and aimed for the lawn in front of the house they were using.

Cole looked up and laughed as his vision blurred with water. 'That was dumb.' He blinked the rain out of his eyes. 'But I think you're right. How long will it take for this new river to go down?'

'If we don't get another deluge I reckon less than twenty-four hours.'

'Now all we have left to do is get Karen out of here.' Cole looked around and was shocked to realise that the sky was lightening. The night was over. What a night it had been. Nothing like he'd expected when leaving Sydney yesterday. Yet he didn't feel any regret. This was why he'd studied medicine in the first place, to help those in dire situations. Okay, some regret, because he and Vicki hadn't had a lot of time alone together, and they definitely needed to. But it could be that just being together, working with their patients, had been good for them. They'd seen another side to each other. They hadn't argued, or withdrawn into themselves.

'Cole,' Vicki called from the house. 'Want to give me a hand? A baby's about to arrive.'

Wow. No matter how bad things got, there were the wonderful moments too. 'Coming. Those contractions sped up?'

'Karen suddenly had a huge meltdown. She needs to be with her boys, and wants her husband here, not in Western Australia. Then baby started getting on with the process, like it's got the message that Mum needs someone of her own right now.'

He couldn't help himself. He wound an arm around his wife's shoulders, hugged her lithe body in against him. Wonderful. Happiness rose, filled him. He was holding Vicki. She'd probably step away in a moment but he'd take what he could get. 'I've got news for her,' he said, breathing deep to savour Vicki's sweet fragrance. He'd missed talking to her, sharing jokes and laughter, and lying in bed with their bodies entwined. 'Good news.'

'Has Lucas come round?' Vicki asked, glancing up at him.

'I wish.' He also wished he could read total uncompromised love in those beautiful eyes. But he couldn't. Wasn't quite sure what he was seeing. Still with his arm around her, he took Vicki inside.

'Karen's in the first bedroom down the hall.'

'Right.' The moment he saw Karen, he said, 'I've been told to let you know that your husband is on his way from Perth right now. The reason you weren't getting through to him was because he's in the air, heading east. He heard about the flooding from his parents hours ago.'

'You're sure?' Hope flicked through her eyes.

'The message came via the rescue doctor from your in-laws. It's going to take time to get to Cairns as he couldn't get the flights he needed.'

'He's coming. That's all that matters. Thank you so much.' Some of the anxiety left her tight face. 'That's wonderful.'

Vicki slipped from under his arm, nodding. 'It is. Now you can relax and let this little one make a grand entrance, then you'll have something to show off to your man when he gets to town.' Her voice was clipped, filled with an emotion Cole didn't like. Sadness. And loneliness.

'I'm sorry,' he said quietly. 'It won't happen again.'

CHAPTER EIGHT

'IT WON'T HAPPEN AGAIN,' Cole repeated under his breath.

He'd never meant anything so much other than telling Vicki he loved her. He used to tell her often, it hadn't been something to be reticent about. It was true, so therefore he told her regularly. Except not for a long time prior to the miscarriage, and definitely not during the last few phone conversations. The atmosphere had become uncomfortable, making him feel if he uttered those words once more she'd think he was deliberately trying to get her onside without going over what had pushed them apart in the first place.

Vicki was too busy taking obs on Karen to give him a smile. Deliberately too busy? Her focus was completely on her patient, though he saw worry filter through her gaze.

'Here we go again.' Karen stood awkwardly and reached for Vicki's hands, clinging to them as the contraction tore through her belly. 'Getting worse.'

'Getting closer.' Vicki smiled tightly. 'I need to re-examine you, see what's going on.'

'The baby's coming, that's what's happening,' Karen growled through gritted teeth.

'Then let's find out where he's at,' Vicki suggested in a firm, don't-argue tone. 'What is it with you and boys anyway? Haven't you heard of girls?'

Karen relaxed a little and sank onto the bed that had been made available by Ester. 'Everyone asks me that, but I'm happy with my sons. It's never bothered me not having a daughter. It's easier having them all the same sex. Though Arlo would've liked a girl. He'd have spoilt her rotten. Oh, that's too soon.' Her face scrunched up in agony and her hands clasped together around her belly.

'Hopefully, this will be over quickly,' Cole said. 'Do you want me here, or should I go look busy elsewhere?'

'You can stay. Though Vicki's doing a great job.'

Vicki chuckled. 'It's you doing all the work and making things easier.'

'Lots of practice,' Karen grunted. 'I swear this is the last time. Four kids are enough.'

'When the contraction ends, can you lie back

and let me see if baby's head's crowning?' Vicki slipped gloves on and handed Cole a pair. 'You up to date with deliveries?'

He was back in favour, as a doctor if nothing else. Then she smiled at him, and his heart turned to mush. More than a doctor then. 'Not a lot of those in the army, but who can forget the amazement of a new baby? I'll never forget the first birth I witnessed as a trainee. The most fantastic experience.'

'I know what you mean.' Her smile remained so she wasn't thinking about the baby they'd lost. 'Sometimes I wonder if I should've done midwifery, but then I think how much I enjoy what I do and it's all good. More variety.'

His heart did a happy dance. For now all was good in his world. 'You ready for this, Karen?'

'As long as you're going to tell me you can see baby.'

'We'll do our best,' he agreed. 'Have you and Arlo chosen a name yet?'

'We've always waited until we've met our boys before deciding on one. I don't know if it's about finding a name that suits or about not wanting to jinx anything, but that's how it's been from when I was pregnant with Lucas.' Mentioning her eldest brought the tears on, and her bottom lip was in danger of being torn by her teeth.

Vicki was quick to take her hands. 'Come on. He's tough. You told me that yourself. His grandparents are at the hospital and shortly all the boys will be there. Soon their dad will be too. The doctors will be doing everything possible to make Lucas well.'

'I—know,' Karen hiccupped. 'But I feel so useless right now. *I'm* his mother. I should've been able to save him from getting hurt. Same for Toby and Callum. Instead I was in the room that suffered the least damage.'

Cole locked a firm gaze on her. 'No one knew that hill would come down, let alone which building it would hit. Certainly, no one had a clue which rooms it would take out. Spare yourself this agony and concentrate on getting your new wee man safely out into the world. All right?'

'Yes.' She swallowed hard. 'I needed that.'

'No problem. We understand what you're going through, but the best thing you can do is stay focused on what's happening here. Once baby's born we can concentrate on getting you both to hospital to join your family.'

Vicki nodded, and moved closer to him, reached for his glove-covered hand, gave him a squeeze. 'You're right. About everything you mentioned.'

As in they both understood Karen's pain? Yes,

they did. It had been a different scenario but the pain of not being there for each other had been real. He squeezed back, wishing he had time to hug Vicki tight. Unfortunately, there was a baby waiting to introduce himself to his mother and that really was as important right now. He gave her one anyway, smiled when she leaned into him briefly.

Vicki said to Karen, 'I'll take a look now.'

It didn't take a second to understand that baby was well and truly on his way, Cole saw. 'You're about to become a mum again. Push, Karen.'

'Strange but I haven't felt the need to do that yet.'

'Maybe not, but give it your best shot.'

He watched Vicki encouraging Karen to push harder. She was gentle and compassionate, yet not letting Karen off doing the hard work required.

Within minutes the room was filled with a delightful cry that tugged at Cole's heartstrings. One day he would be a dad. When Vicki had told him she was pregnant he'd been ecstatic. They were going to be parents, raise their own child, love him or her to bits, share the good and bad times, always be there to support him or her through everything the world threw their way. Believe in their honesty.

Then the dream had imploded. It was a common occurrence for parents-to-be, but not once had he realised how devastating it would be when it happened to them. He'd buried the despair while in hospital and only recently had he taken out the anguish of the miscarriage and thought it through. It hurt, but not as much as losing Vicki would.

'Let me hold him,' Karen squealed, holding her arms out to take the precious bundle he held in his large hands, making the tiny tot look even smaller.

He didn't want to let the baby go, wanted to feel the warm, wriggling body in his palms. Of course he handed him over, watched Karen snuggle her new son against her breasts. One day. He glanced sideways and saw the amazed expression on Vicki's face. Reaching for her hand again, he gave another squeeze. Definitely one day.

When she leaned close to lay her head against his shoulder he couldn't hold back a smile. Or the kiss he dropped on her forehead. This felt right, just like them, and encouraged him to think all was not lost.

'We know how to pick our weekend, don't we?'

Vicki dropped her sodden jacket on the laundry floor, then shucked out of her shorts. Not a good idea, if that gleam in Cole's eyes meant what she thought it did. Why would she be wrong, having seen it often in the past? Too late. She wasn't going to pull the pants back on. That would only make them both more aware of each other.

Who am I kidding? I couldn't be more conscious of Cole if I tried.

So she had to divert his interest. 'Here's hoping the rest of today and tomorrow are ours to use as we choose.'

Going by the way Cole's eyes widened, that wasn't working as a distraction. Seemed he had ideas about how he wanted to use their time together. 'Yeah, I'm hoping we've done our bit for the community. I'd like to spend time with you and no one else.'

'Me, too,' she admitted, remembering the gentle kiss on her forehead that had turned her toes to mush. 'But I confess I'm exhausted.' She'd had very little sleep the night before last, none last night, her nerves on edge for days over Cole coming, and there wasn't much oomph left inside her. Seriously? When the man of her heart stood before her? What was wrong with her? They still had a few problems yet to sort out. Her shoulders slumped. 'I'm going to have a shower, then some breakfast. Or lunch,' she added after seeing her mother's ancient wall clock showing ten forty-five.

'So am I,' he agreed, his eyes finally settling back to normal and a smile appearing. 'Let's go with brunch. Covers all the bases.'

'Sounds good.' Especially if Cole was cooking. Was she wrong to leave the order of things the same, or should she be stepping up more? The problem was she liked slipping back into their routine. It gave her confidence they'd work everything out in a good way. 'Where did the hours go?'

'Into boys and a baby, and hanging around waiting to get out of the place.'

'There was a time I started to wonder if we'd ever be brought back over to our side.' They'd waited more than an hour to be brought across the flood waters and driven home.

'You don't think Damon or Merv would've left you there any longer than they had to, do you?' Cole smiled. 'Not when Damon was on edge about you being anywhere near that moving hillside.'

'True. I suppose that second house getting swamped with mud and water ruined his plans for excavating us sooner rather than later.' Cole was still staring at her like he'd forgotten what her legs looked like. Grabbing a towel off the shelf, she wrapped it around her waist, and smiled to herself when he sucked a breath and looked away.

'I'm glad we were able to help those people, but I'm hoping that's the end of it this weekend.' Was it selfish to think she'd rather have spent time with Cole, sorting out their differences? Probably, but it showed she was human, didn't it?

'You're a confident nurse, and the patients respond well to you.'

Wow. A low laugh bubbled through her, followed by a wave of warmth that wrapped around her heart. 'I could say the same about you, Doctor. We did well in a tough situation. That house gave me the creeps. I kept hearing the walls and roof creaking and cracking, and expected it to drop on my head any moment.'

'The guys did a good job of shoring it up, at least for long enough to evacuate the family. Who knows what state the house will be in later today.'

'It's an insurance job, that one.'

'There'll be a few of those after this.' Cole ran his finger across her chin. 'I did enjoy being with you, despite the circumstances. We still fit well together.'

She locked her eyes with his steady, endearing gaze. 'You're right.' She swayed towards him, and couldn't find the brakes to stop. Lifting her arms, she wound them around his neck. 'It's been quite a night.' She had no idea where she was, other than holding Cole, being so close to him, needing him. Loving him.

His head came closer, his lips brushing hers before whispering, 'Vicki, love.' Then he was kissing her, deeply, lovingly.

Rising onto her toes, she pushed against his chest, kissed him back, her tongue darting into his mouth to taste. She had missed this, him, so much it had hurt. And heated her blood as she continued to return his kisses. 'Cole,' she murmured against his mouth as his hands spread across her waist.

He lifted her, sat her on top of the washing machine, pushed his hips between her legs, and continued kissing, continued ramping up her desire, turning her body into an inferno of need. This was them. This was how they'd got back together every time he'd been away.

This was bad timing. They hadn't resolved a thing yet, and as much as making love would be wonderful, it might make keeping on track that much harder. Reluctance warred with need as she pulled her mouth away. She so didn't want to stop. But she had to if she was to be true to herself. Which she had to be. Or else lose everything. 'Cole.'

His eyes flew open, dark and excited with lust. 'Sweetheart?'

'I'm sorry.'

He blew out a lungful of air and stared at her, his disappointment so strong she nearly changed her mind. 'Me, too.' He didn't drop his hands from her waist straight away, stood there, holding her, watching her with such tenderness in his gaze she felt tears building up.

As she opened her mouth to apologise again, he placed a finger on her lips.

'Don't. You're right. We've some things to resolve first.' Then he brushed a light kiss on her cheek. 'But I'd be lying if I said I didn't enjoy that and wasn't hanging out for more.'

He knew how to make her feel better about what she'd done. She blinked, risked a smile. 'It's not just in the medical field we work well together.'

His eyes widened and he actually laughed. 'Never a truer word. Here...' He lifted her down. 'Go get out of the rest of those wet clothes and take a shower.'

'More water? Just what I need.' She grinned. Somehow she was comfortable, despite what had just gone down. 'See you in the kitchen soon.' She wasn't about to say that if she didn't make it to brunch he'd better look for her as she might be asleep in the shower. After that kiss, he'd be there before the water got warm, let alone cold again. She'd not be able to stop him. How she'd pulled away at all stumped her.

She'd been ready for Cole to make love to her, to give back as good as she got.

Glancing outside, she saw that the sun was heading up the sky, peeking through gaps in the clouds, trying its best to turn the gloom into refreshing light. The rain had eased to a heavy drizzle, but Damon had warned the monsoon might not be over, could be gathering strength for a final deluge. There was water every darned where. Roads, parks and fields were drowned. Here at Palm Beach homeowners had been lucky so far. No buildings were flooded. Once the storm was over, it would take days for the area to dry out. Weather like this was one of the few aspects of living in Northern Queensland she hadn't missed when she'd headed south to Sydney.

Under a cool temperature in the shower she scrubbed mud off all her skin that had been exposed throughout the night, and some that hadn't. How had it got under her bra and waistband? When she shampooed her hair, brown suds filled the shower base. Hopefully, there was some softening element in mud that was good for skin and hair. Bending her head under the shower head, she leaned against the wall and let the warm water rinse her hair thoroughly. One yawn followed another, and another.

She would fall asleep if she wasn't careful.

Then Cole would come to find her. That was not happening. Pushing the lever off, she reached for her towel. Had a moment where she imagined Cole handing it to her. Her eyes snapped open. Nope. She was alone.

Wrapping the towel around her, she dashed to the bedroom and thought about diving under the covers, but the smell of frying bacon coming from down the hall was too tantalising to be ignored. Pulling on shorts and tee shirt, she began brushing the tangled knots out of her hair. Hopefully, it would dry before she hit the sack because she couldn't be bothered getting out the dryer and styling the long, straight cut. If it looked too bad when she got up later she'd deal to it then.

'How many eggs?' Cole called from the other side of the bedroom door.

'Two.'

'Going on now.'

'I'm coming.'

Were they going to have a relaxed brunch? She hoped so. Spending time together working with people who needed their medical skills had done wonders to her stress levels. She could see herself living with Cole again with certain changes. Long talks with Julie had opened her eyes beyond the wake-up call her mother had given her. Until that time with her sister, Vicki hadn't understood why Julie had deliberately gone so far away so as not to repeat their mother's life.

And now I have to stick to my guns and do the same.

'Take a load off.' Cole pointed to a comfy cane chair in the covered outdoor area near the barbecue.

'I'll make some tea first.' That thick cushion looked tempting, but once she sank into it she'd not want to get up again.

'All done. Here.' He handed her a brimming mug.

'You must've had a quick shower to have got all this ready.' There was cutlery and plates, sauces and seasonings on the table. Bacon sizzled alongside the hash browns and tomatoes, eggs and mushrooms were coming up to speed on the second hot plate. She should've been getting everything ready while Cole cooked, not lazing in the shower.

Cole grinned. 'Thought I was going to have to come in with a bucket of icy water to wake you up.'

'That would not have won you any favours.' She laughed, relaxing some more. Sitting, she sipped the tea. 'I suppose the next thing will be to get out and help people clean up the debris from yards where the waters have gone through.'

'That won't begin until the flood's receded. A couple of days away, I imagine. It's going to be a busy time for everyone.' Cole began filling a plate with the most delicious-smelling food she'd had in a long time.

'I've always been amazed at how quickly everyone gets back to normal. Except for those whose properties are damaged, of course. Still haven't heard from Phil. The boys in blue must be busy.'

Cole placed a laden plate on the table in front of her. 'Here you go. Get that into you.'

'Yummy. Thanks.'

'I have my uses.'

Her face heated. The number of times he'd said that to her over the years. It usually referred to time in bed, and nothing to do with sleeping. Concentrating on eating, Vicki managed to avoid looking directly at her husband until images of them making love finally faded. All she had to do was reach across the gap between them and entwine her fingers with his, and they'd be heading down the hall. Maybe getting up close and sexy would help, and they could laugh for getting so stressed about their marriage.

'Hey, don't go to sleep in your brunch,' Cole goaded her deliberately. 'Egg on face is not pretty.'

Sleep was the last thing on her mind. Unfortunately. She glanced across the table, and sighed at Cole's cheeky grin. 'Then you'd better wipe your chin.'

He did, then laughed when he saw there was nothing on the napkin. 'Wretch.'

'Don't you forget it.' She pushed her empty plate aside. 'Just what the doctor ordered.'

'Just what the doctor cooked, you mean.'

'And that.'

Cole wiped his plate clean and leaned back in his chair. He nodded in the direction of the lounge. 'I like that painting of the Daintree. It's new, isn't it?'

'It's one of Mum's. She's getting better with each painting. I can't wait to see what she brings back from this trip.'

'Anna's painting while on the road?'

'She's working on a series of coastal pictures. Mostly she's taking a million photos and notes to use when she's back home.' Pride filled Vicki. Her mother was already achieving recognition. 'The city gallery wants to put on a small show of her work next year and she's panicking about getting enough done. Says she'll lose her edge if she rushes the work. I don't believe she will. It's like a tap's been turned on and there's no stopping her.'

'I can't believe she's waited so long to get back into following her passion,' Cole commented.

I can. And if I'm not careful I'll have the same regrets when I reach my fifties. Agency, here I come.

'At least she's doing it now.'

Her contribution towards getting her mother started must've helped. The day she'd put that easel, those paints and brushes in the lounge, ready for when her mother came home, she'd waited with a beating heart, afraid of having done the wrong thing, and that her mother might tell her off for raising her hopes. But when her mother had picked up a brush, a look of wonder on her face, she'd known she'd got it right. Then denial had hit and instantly Vicki had stepped up and pressed the brush firmly back into her mum's hand and wrapped her fingers around the handle.

You can do it, Mum. You have to. And so can I.

'Why did she wait so long?'

'Four kids and Dad's demanding medical practice, I guess.'

I know.

'I get that, but couldn't she have found some time for herself? A few hours here and there between washing the dirty clothes and baking the biscuits?'

'Cole, that sounds like it was a hobby to fill in spare time. Mum has a special talent, and she did not want to give it a nodding glance. It was all or nothing, and because she'd committed to Dad and us it became nothing.'

'My mother was a bit like that too. Must be a generational thing.' He gathered up their plates and stood. 'Want more tea?'

'I'll get it, and clean up.' Wasn't that how she used to respond?

'Stay there. You look whacked.'

'Okay, thanks.' That was better. Whacked didn't describe how she felt. Behind the eyes there was a battle going on between falling asleep and telling Cole what she thought about his comment. 'It was quite a night.' Generational thing, like hell. He really didn't get what her mother had given up for her family. And if his mother had done the same, no wonder he'd thought it was normal. She hadn't done anything different to show she wasn't sitting around not getting on with her dreams either. 'So, back to full-time medicine, huh?'

A full mug appeared before her. 'Like I said, I'd like to go into general practice, leave the emergency scene behind. I've seen enough to know I'd prefer being in a position where I get to know my patients a little.' Cole began wiping down the barbecue. 'To have the whole picture, understand what drives them, how they live, where they work. Know the whole family. That sort of thing.'

'The complete opposite from working in ED then.' Her agency would hire out temps to his practice. Her mouth tipped into a small smile. This could work. She yawned. It was unbelievable how tired she felt. Another yawn. The tea warmed her even though she wasn't cold. Or was that Cole's presence? 'I've got some ideas for my career I'm working on that's different to what I've been doing, too.'

'Not retraining as a midwife? I didn't think you wanted to do that.'

'No. I'm looking at setting up my own nursing agency.' She held her breath, waiting for the quiz.

'You'd be good at that, organising people to do jobs, keeping staff busy and happy, getting them on board in the first place.' Cole nodded as he lowered the hood of the barbecue.

Knock me down.

'You were supposed be shocked and tell me I'm nuts.' Instead she was the one shocked.

He smiled. 'I figured.' Then he came over to drop into the seat opposite her.

'I've always thought about one day having my own agency, but I put it on hold when we married. Then one week last year when we were so busy at the emergency department, everyone doing extra shifts because there was a staff shortage due to a viral outbreak in the city, I started thinking about it again.'

'Don't the agencies already out there provide enough nurses?'

'It'll be a challenge, but it's one I want to do. I feel this is something I would be good at.' She stared at Cole. 'It's not a pipe dream. I've been looking into all the aspects a business like that requires. I can do it.'

'I believe you can, too.'

'Really?'

'Really.'

He still hadn't asked why she hadn't mentioned it before. Were they more alike than she'd realised? Vicki gasped. Yes, they were. Here she'd been getting upset because he hadn't told her about the accident and yet she'd kept the agency idea to herself after that one time years ago.

That was slightly different.

She hadn't started it up yet. The plans were coming together but she hadn't put anything in place to shackle him with. If she'd been open, would he have been more so about his accident? And other things? Something else she'd probably never have an answer to. 'You don't remember me mentioning it years ago?'

Looking baffled, Cole shook his head. 'No, I don't.'

Just as she'd thought. 'Maybe I should've reminded you.'

'Let's not argue over this. The important thing is I now know and can support you.'

Gulp. It was that simple? Go with it. 'Thanks, da—Cole.' She nearly said *darling*. Actually, now that she'd got the agency thing out in the open, maybe she should've. He wasn't running for the hills, or telling her it was all impossible because it wouldn't fit in with his plans. Things were looking up.

CHAPTER NINE

VICKI HAD BEEN thinking about setting up her own agency? For that long? Cole shook his head to clear the surprise. He hadn't had a clue that she might want to do something different, especially starting her own business. She loved nursing, always said it kept her grounded in reality with the wonderful and awful cases she'd worked. 'What about nursing? If you're running an agency there won't be time for any of that.'

'At first I'll still be working. I'll need the money, and I won't be as busy as you're suggesting. It's going to take time to establish my name and get medical centres to call me instead of their usual source of temporary nurses.'

She wasn't acting overly confident, but seemed to have worked out some of the pitfalls at least. A good sign. 'Don't worry about start-up money. We'll sort that between us.' Why hadn't she mentioned it way back before they'd begun falling apart?

Embarrassment crept across Vicki's face. 'It wasn't a hint for you to help me out.'

'Didn't cross my mind you'd stoop to that. It's a genuine offer.' He wasn't asking if she wanted him on board with this, or with their marriage. He would continue to believe in them and act accordingly unless she put the brakes on. Then he'd fight tooth and nail for what they'd once had.

'Thanks.' The embarrassment deepened, her cheeks reddening.

'Vicki, we can make this work. I mean everything.'

She nodded. 'We were once strong together. Seems we've got a little lost this past year, but hopefully nothing we can't fix with a little patience.' She was drawing circles on the tabletop with her forefinger, getting faster all the time. 'I'm not going to change my mind about this agency, Cole. I want to achieve something for myself, something to be proud of.'

'Then you will. There's nothing stopping you.'

Especially not me.

Where did she want to set this up? Here in Cairns with her family nearby, or back in Sydney where they owned an apartment and their closest friends resided? Where they'd established their life after marrying? Except he hadn't been there often enough. What about the job he was close to obtaining? Nothing seemed straight-forward.

Surprise replaced her embarrassment. 'You think?'

Ouch. 'Don't you know I believe in you?'

'I think it's more that I don't believe in myself as much as I need to.'

'Where does that come from? You're always confident. Look how you've managed in Sydney while I've been away. That took guts and strength.'

Her head came up instantly, and the eyes that locked on him were glittery. 'It did, and it wasn't enough.'

They were back at the beginning. At why they'd got themselves into this mess. Reaching for her hands, he gripped tight. 'You became lonely. I get that, though you did a good job of hiding it from me in the early years.'

She nodded. 'At first it was fine. I managed, I was supporting you, and I had friends to spend time with. Then the wheels started coming off, and I couldn't seem to stop the bus.'

'Nice way with words.' He smiled, though his heart was stuttering. He wanted to believe they were moving forward together, but he couldn't help the sense of not quite understanding everything she was telling him. For every step forward there was at least another one backwards. 'Where's the bus now?'

She pulled her hands free and leaned back. 'It's beginning to turn around.' Then her face collapsed, tearing him in two. 'Oh, Cole. What have we done?'

'Nothing that can't be fixed, sweetheart.'

'I hope you're right.'

That was the first hint she might want the same as he did. He wouldn't let the hope get out of control. 'I'm damned sure of it.' Lifting her hands again, he kissed her white knuckles. 'Promise.'

At last a smile crept over her mouth. 'I'll second that.' She slumped in her chair, as though all the energy had evaporated out of her. Not that she'd been hyperactive since they'd returned from helping Karen and her family.

A phone rang. 'That's mine,' Cole said, and dug it out of his pocket, in need of a break while he digested everything Vicki had hit him with. 'Hey, Nathan, how's things down there?'

Vicki sank further into her chair, her eyelids drooping. As though now she'd let out about the agency she could relax. 'Say hi to Molly for me.'

'More like, how's things up in Cairns?' Nathan asked. 'Apart from wet?'

'Busy.'

Not in the way I'd expected.

'Vicki and I were called out to an old guy who'd taken a tumble off his ladder late yesterday, then we spent all night working with a family trapped in their house.' He went on to explain what had happened, and watched Vicki's eyes slowly closing and her chin dropping onto her sternum. She was shattered. It wasn't like her at all.

'Suppose that means you haven't had time to tell her your plans for down here,' Nathan said when he'd finished.

Crossing to the window, he stared out. Those plans were up in the air now, apart from the interview on Monday that might mean he had a position in a very good medical centre. He huffed out a deep breath. 'There hasn't been much time to sit down and go through whatever's bugging Vicki, apart from me being absent so much. At least she knows that's over for good.' He wasn't mentioning her nursing agency while he was still getting his head around it. 'She says hi to Molly, by the way.'

'Moll wants to talk to her when we're done.'

Cole looked back at his wife. 'Not happening. She's fallen asleep in the short time we've been talking.' What was left of her tea was in danger of spilling over her thighs. He stepped across to retrieve the mug, hoping not to wake her. She didn't move, even when he lifted her fingers from the handle. His heart lurched at the unguarded expression on her face. She looked so fragile. There were so many sides to this woman, and he loved them all. Right now he wanted to hold her and promise she was never going to have to worry about him letting her down again.

After finishing talking to Nathan, he headed down to Vicki's bedroom to pull back the covers on the bed. Returning, he scooped her up into his arms, ignoring the tug on his spine where a niggling ache still made itself known. Back in the bedroom he gently laid her down on her side and pulled the sheet up to her chin. Still she didn't move.

He stood watching her, feeling his love ballooning, filling him, making him believe the future would be great. They'd replace the apartment with a house and fill the bedrooms with kids. Get another dog. He'd make her happy.

What if she wouldn't have him back? What if the agency was to replace him? Something to keep her focused because she didn't believe he was home for good? Sydney or Cairns? The niggling questions sent a cold fear through him. It might be a short-lived belief their future was safe. But they had so much to give each other.

'Cole?' Vicki muttered in her sleep.

So she hadn't stopped thinking about him

while she slept. 'I'm here, sweetheart.' But he'd head off for a snooze so that he'd be on full alert later when they sat down together. To talk about things like how soon could she join him in Sydney? If she was prepared to return there? Why not set up her business there where there was larger scope of medical places to work with?

'I love you, Vicki. Always have, always will.' His chest expanded, ignoring the caution that he might be rushing this. That he might've got it wrong, and there was a lot more Vicki wasn't happy about. Apart from him being away so much, especially when disasters had struck, she hadn't said anything else had been wrong with their relationship.

Sitting on the edge of the bed, he let the memories come. Their honeymoon in Rarotonga. The excitement when they'd bought the apartment and moved in with only a bed for furniture. Meeting Benji for the first time, and instantly falling in love with his big brown, beguiling eyes. Those plastic flowers. They had history; good, binding, loving history. Too much to let go.

Vicki rolled his way, muttering, 'Cole...' again.

He lay down beside her, not touching her, barely breathing, needing to be close, afraid she'd wake up and yell at him to get away.

But suddenly her arm was wrapping over his chest, and she shuffled closer so her head was against his arm. Carefully, so as not to wake her, he slid his hand into hers and breathed slowly. Damn, how he'd missed this. Another of those simple acts that held so much love and understanding. He relaxed as her scent reached him, and listened to her steady breathing. And continued delving through those memories. Enjoying the good times and ignoring the nagging feeling there was more bad to come. That he'd missed something important.

Vicki smiled as she slowly drifted awake. Everything felt right with her world. Cole's arm was tucked around her waist, his chest and stomach pressed against her back, his legs touching hers, as his light breaths tickled her neck. She savoured the moment. As she became aware of his arousal heat flooded her body, brought her to wide awake in an instant. 'Cole?' she whispered.

His arm tightened around her, and he kissed the back of her neck, setting her skin tight. 'Hey.'

She tried to roll over.

'Don't.' His mouth trailed further over her neck and to her shoulder.

Reaching behind, her hand found his hip and slid beyond to his butt, where her fingers worked their magic on his sexy, smooth skin. Against her backside Cole's arousal hardened. Then she attempted to push between them to wrap her hand around him.

'No,' he whispered. 'Let me make love to you first.' His hand caressed her breasts, first one until it ached, then the other, her nipples almost exploding with tension.

Somehow she managed to remove her clothes. Then she was pushing at Cole's shorts and finally he paused briefly to get rid of them before he returned to circling her nipple while his other hand cupped her sex. And took her straight to the edge. Typical, she acknowledged happily.

'Now. Hurry. I can't wait,' she gasped through the haze of need clawing through her. 'I want you.'

I've never stopped wanting you.

'I'm here, sweetheart.' And he was, entering her, hard and fast, and they were as one in the best way imaginable. Moving with abandon, Vicki let go all the restraints and worries of the previous months and joined Cole in just being them.

Her face split into a wide grin as she rolled onto her back and regained her breath. Over before they'd begun. Giving, taking, knowing which buttons to push. It was always like this the first time they made love when Cole came home. Later they'd do it again, except they'd take time to touch everywhere with fingers and tongues, building up the intensity, letting it roll through them in soft waves that slowly built up and up until neither could bear not having the release they sought.

Reaching out, she ran her hand down Cole's chest, over his abs and beyond. Hang on. What was that? Running her fingers over his abs again, then further to the side, she felt a ridge. A scar? One of his injuries?

She sat up, her mouth drying. There was a scar where his spleen had been removed. Trailing her gaze downward, she took in more harsh purple lines on his leg. Leaning closer, she gently ran her fingers over each.

'Cole, darling…'

Then she couldn't say any more, her throat blocked with the tears she fought not to shed, her heart beating against her ribs. What if the accident had been worse? What if—? What if a hundred things.

'Stop, Vicki. None of it happened. I'm here, and in relatively good nick.' He lifted her hand away and kissed her fingertips one at a time.

'But—' She should've been with him. Would've been. If he'd told her, asked for her.

Woulda, shoulda, coulda.

They couldn't go back and undo a thing.

What had happened had happened. End of. But it wasn't. The glow receded.

'No buts. Like I said, I survived.'

Swinging her legs over the side of the bed, she stood and picked up her clothes. 'Thank goodness for that.'

Cole sat up, and reached for her. 'Stop torturing yourself, please.'

She stepped back. 'I'm trying but it's not as straightforward as I'd thought.' There were so many reasons for walking into his arms and moving on. But she was held back by nagging doubts she couldn't define. 'Where do we go from here, Cole? You say you want to be a GP. It's great you've got plans for your career, as I have.'

'We can support each other in these choices.'

She was hearing the man who didn't tell her everything. 'Have you been looking for a position?'

He stepped into his shorts and zipped them up. 'Yes. It filled in time while I was incapacitated. Neither did I want to sit around filling in crossword puzzles when I could be making major decisions about my career.'

Anger won out. 'Come on, Cole. Tell me what's going on. At the moment it seems like nothing's changed. You're making plans without involving me.'

There was reciprocal anger in the eyes that locked on her. 'And you haven't done the same?'

A strange sense of almost relief hit her. At last he wasn't trying to placate her about everything, might finally be beginning to show what mattered to him. 'To a certain extent I have, yes.'

'You either have or haven't, Vicki.' He stepped past her through the doorway and headed down the hall.

Following, she ended up on the deck where he stood, hands on hips, staring out to the road, chin thrust forward. Wanting to escape her? Not until he told her what he had done about a job, he wasn't. Because now she suspected he'd already found a position somewhere in Sydney. Which was fine, if only they'd discussed it first. She should have some say in where they'd live if they were to remain married.

Suddenly, he spun around. 'Which is it, Vicki?'

It was her turn to stare out. The rain had eased even more, but the yard still looked like a toddler's paddling pool. 'Having my own agency is not negotiable.' Guess that sounded like she was doing her own thing without involving Cole.

Well, aren't you?

Her stomach churned. To think a short time ago they'd made love like they didn't have a problem between them. There wouldn't be the follow-up long and slow lovemaking session. Not yet, possibly never. 'I've looked into the financial side of setting it up here and in Sydney. Likewise the feasibility of employing nurses, and the medical centres and emergency rooms that might use my agency.'

'Where have you decided on?' he ground out.

'I haven't come to a final conclusion.' This was where she should be saying she'd been waiting to talk to him about it and make a joint decision about where they lived. But she was equally riled up now. 'Cairns would be a lot easier. I know a lot of people here, whereas in Sydney—well, the population's enormous.'

'Why is this so important now? Why not four years ago when I signed up for the military and you apparently told me? That would've kept you busy and left no time to be lonely.'

'We were newlyweds and I was busy making a home for us and being there for you whenever you came home. Don't forget we were living in the married quarters until you went offshore the first time and I chose to return to our apartment.

'You could've run an agency from anywhere. Still can.' He wasn't buying it. Also ignoring the reminder she'd given.

'At the time I had my dream job in the emergency department so thought I'd wait a bit.'

'You—'

She stabbed the air between them with her finger. 'Hear me out. After the miscarriage I couldn't face going into the department every day, pretending all was fine in my world. It was nowhere near. By then I'd been looking into this idea of mine more thoroughly. When I got pregnant…' *gulp* '…it seemed a great way to still be actively working while at the same time being a stay-at-home mum. For once I was thinking about doing what was important for me. As well as you.'

'That sounds like an afterthought. You working while raising a child when I can afford for you not to work doesn't add up to me, and doesn't tie in with any ideas we had when we talked about having a family.' Cole was still watching her intently.

'What about my own self-worth? Doing something that I get enjoyment from? I don't want to get to my fifties and realise I haven't followed my dreams too.' She nodded. 'I know I'd get that from being a mum if I carried a baby to full term.' She hesitated. That was a question she'd refused to consider before. But seeing Cole's bewilderment at her ideas made her face up to reality.

Instantly, his expression softened. 'Miscarriages are common, and most women go on to have normal pregnancies.'

'The nurse in me knows that. The want-to-be mum has doubts.'

'A perfectly normal reaction.'

Her smile was tentative. Were they getting back on side? 'So I'm normal. Thank goodness for something.'

'Did I say that?' Cole smiled back. 'Not too normal. That'd be boring, and the last thing you are is boring.'

This was all very good but once again they hadn't finished the discussion that had started with what Cole had done about getting a position in a medical centre. 'Where do you intend working?'

'I'd thought Sydney because that's where we live. Lived.'

Nice to have mentioned it. 'Have you applied for a place yet?'

'I've got a third and, hopefully, final interview at a medical centre near Rose Bay first thing Monday morning. The partners have intimated the position will probably be mine. It's quite exciting, and so different from anything I've done before. We could find a house in the area, and even have a boat since the harbour's on the doorstep.'

Bang. Exactly as she'd thought. It was like a fist to the heart. Sydney, whether they agreed or not. Discussed it or not. Added in her requirements or not. Where was the heads together, talk about the pros and cons discussion? 'Did you come here to tell me you're going to live and work in Sydney regardless of what I thought?'

'Jeez, Vicki, give me a break here. I came because I love you and want to get back together.'

'In Sydney. Near Rose Bay, to be precise.'

'Yes, because that's where I'll probably have a job.' His excitement was waning. Beginning to understand she mightn't be rushing to join him wherever he chose. That the divorce was for real.

'Did it never occur to you to tell me what you were aiming for? Before you went to your first interview?'

'We hadn't been talking a lot.'

'That's pathetic, Cole. You never even tried to tell me. No wonder this isn't working. You still expect me to toe the line. Sure, I can have my own business—it just has to be where you decide.' She stared at him, shaking her head in frustration. 'I don't believe this.'

Yet she should. Nothing had changed. Not really, despite everything he'd said this weekend about them being together.

'Here I was, waiting until we'd worked out if we were still together and then where *we'd* live before making my final decision on where to set up the agency, and all the while you've gone ahead with your own plans. That's not togetherness, Cole. That's me following you around again. Even if you're not going away any more, I'm a partner in our marriage. Or I was.'

Stop. Right. Now. Too much.

But it was how she felt. Hurt, disappointed, humiliated even. She wouldn't be accused of not telling Cole what she thought. Not now or later, if there was going to be a later.

Cole sank onto a chair and dropped his head in his hands. 'I thought you'd be pleased I was settling into a long-term job in the city where we've always been happy. It was supposed to make you feel sure of me and my motives. Look, I'm here for good, no leaving you to carry all the hard stuff on your own any more.'

The genuineness behind his statement rang loud and clear between them. It still didn't make the situation acceptable. Vicki pulled out another chair and sat down. Her legs were a bit wobbly and her head was spinning. They'd made wild love as only they could do, kissed until her body melted; laughed, talked, and worked together over the past twenty-four hours. Even argued, spoken of the past and the future, and yet here they were, stuck, unable to move in any direction.

But she wasn't ready to give up trying. Not yet.

'Cole, why do you make decisions that involve

both of us without saying a word to me first?' The shock of finding out one day he'd joined the army still had the capability to rock her at times. He hadn't told her he was actually going to do that either, just mentioned in passing a couple of times that he was interested in finding out more about joining up one day.

He stood up, rolled his shoulders. 'Want a beer? Wine?'

May as well. Nothing else was working. 'Wine would be nice.' She was exhausted. Her body ached everywhere. The banging inside her head was worse than ever. It would be a darned sight easier to give up trying to make Cole see her side of this and just go with the flow. A lot simpler. And a lot more frustrating, which would eventually lead right back to this moment.

Cole returned with their drinks and a plate with Brie and crackers. The nibbles weren't so much a peace offering as something to quieten his rumbling stomach, which he hoped was caused by hunger and not despair of ever getting things right with Vicki again. Probably kidding himself there.

He didn't sit, instead leaned against one of the pillars holding the roof over the deck and sipped his beer. Vicki was watching him, waiting for an explanation. A long overdue one, true, and still difficult to deliver. More so because he'd shied away from it for so long. But this was the right time. Now or never, and never meant not being able to win Vicki back. 'I did tell you I was accused of stealing some money from a local charity in our town.'

Her gaze didn't waver. 'You were cleared of it. Or so you said.'

'I was.' And that was as much as he'd ever told her.

'I don't understand how you could've been accused in the first place. You're not the kind of person who'd do anything like that.'

Warmth filled him briefly. 'Thank you for that.' He sipped his beer before continuing. 'If only others had reacted the same way. The town was in an uproar, not because the amount of money taken was well over ten thousand dollars but that anyone would steal from the charity at all. That I would. The fact I came from a well-off family seemed to make it a worse crime in *everyone's* eyes.'

'As in your family and friends?'

He nodded abruptly, swallowed the bile that question had brought on. 'At first Mum and Dad accepted I was guilty. Then they began listening to me and finally admitted they'd been wrong. Dad tried to make up for it by ignoring those who believed I was guilty and burying himself in work more than ever. Mum became more withdrawn as the loss of her friends hit home.'

'How did you cope?'

I became someone else.

'My friends, or those I'd believed were friends, added to the misery. We were all together that night.' He explained what had happened. 'I didn't learn how they'd driven my car to the charity room until one of the guys admitted it all eight months later. I was embarrassed, then angry. My girlfriend had put a date drug in my beer. I'd always felt ashamed that I hadn't known what had gone on, and the truth actually increased my shame. I was used.'

Placing her glass back on the table without taking a sip, she again locked her gaze with his. 'That wasn't your fault.'

'True.' He shrugged. 'But how gullible was I to accept a beer that had been drugged?'

'No one knows they've been given date drugs until it's too late.'

'The whole incident taught me to be wary of who I chose for friends.'

'Why are you only telling me this now when it's obvious it's made you who you are?'

There was no holding her back on the tricky questions any more. It seemed the time he'd been away had made her tougher. Which he couldn't fault. At least that had kept her safe from making mistakes. 'It was a horrible time for me and my family, and when I fell in love with you I didn't want to bring it into our lives. It changed me so much. I became wary of trusting people and yet you I totally trusted instantly. It was something I didn't want to spoil. I had no issues with you believing me. It was more that I wanted to be accepted for who I was without all the bull dust attached.'

'So you've never told anyone since it happened?' The hurt tightened her face, darkened her eyes. She didn't accept that he hadn't told her.

Now he was about to make it worse, because he wouldn't lie to Vicki. Not even if it meant she'd hate him. 'Nathan has known for most of our friendship.'

'I see.'

No, she didn't. But he wasn't going to grovel. He and Nathan had met when he'd still been raw from what his so-called friends had done and he'd wanted to test him. Quite the reverse to his decision not to tell Vicki. He should've done it the other way round, but then hindsight was all very well.

'Has this got anything to do with joining the army?'

His sigh was low and sad. 'Mum died before I was proved innocent. I always wondered if the stress killed her. In those desperate hours after her heart attack she apologised for not believing in me and said she was proud of me for being so strong.'

He swallowed as a picture filled his mind of his mother's drawn, white face as she'd lain there, crying and apologising.

'I was seventeen, and my mother was dying before my eyes. I couldn't face that so I promised to make her more proud of me.' A chill settled over him. 'I was trying to keep her alive by giving her something to hold out for. Granddad had been awarded a military medal for his part in active service and she was always going on about him so it seemed the way to go.'

'Why couldn't you have told me that?' Bleak eyes fixed on him. 'I didn't come into the picture at all, did I? How long was I supposed to sit back and wait until you were ready to include me in all aspects of your life?' Her questions were stabs at his heart.

'I got into the habit of not divulging things about myself, not wanting to bring my youth into my adulthood.' He should've known not to do that after the way he'd been treated over the theft. 'I'm so sorry, Vicki.'

She went on in a softer voice. 'To be fair, I did wait quietly in the wings. So I can't get angry at you for that. But I woke up after the miscarriage. I needed you then. More than I've ever needed anyone. That was our baby I lost and you weren't available. I know other women have been through a miscarriage on their own; I never expected it to be me. That was when I understood I do not want a marriage where we're not together most of the time. I grew up having family around me. I can't live without that. I'm sorry too.'

'It won't happen again, I promise. You'll always have me with you. I am not going anywhere without you again.'

'So you say, but you're still making decisions without talking through them with me. I'd thought we'd work this out. I was not expecting more shocks, Cole. I can't handle it. I need time to think it through. You may as well return to Sydney and your interview early.' She stood up and looked at him, sorrow written all over her face. 'I wish this had worked out how we'd both hoped.'

'What do you mean? Are you saying we're over? Our marriage really is finished?' He could hardly utter the words the pain was so horrendous. 'Vicki. Don't do this,' he gasped.

Tears streaked over her cheeks. His beautiful Vicki was hurting as much as him. He stepped forward to take her in his arms, only to be stopped immediately.

'No.' Her breast lifted on a deep breath. 'You need to stop proving to everyone else how strong you are and get on with living a life that's true to you.'

She was right. He had been hiding from so much.

Vicki hadn't finished. 'I'm sorry. I am not ready to return to being a couple. I don't believe we've really been one in the way I thought. So I guess I am saying we're still separating.' Then she turned and left him.

Cole watched her go, heading to her bedroom where they'd made love a short time ago. He could still feel her breasts against his chest, her moist warmth as he'd entered her. Would they ever do that again? Would she give him another chance? Pain lanced him into shreds. Vicki was his woman, the love of his life. It was impossible to accept she believed they were over.

He wasn't going to. Taking a step in her direction, he faltered. He'd said all he could. There was nothing more to add. Vicki had to believe him when he'd said he was always going to be here for her.

But she didn't.

Should he go and grovel? Beg for another chance? Or give her space and time to take in everything he'd told her? If he did that would she ever let him see her again? Ever talk to him again? Fear chilled him, lifted bumps on his skin, closed down the warmth of their lovemaking. They were so close, so far. This could not be happening. But it was.

Vicki believed he was wrong to make decisions without involving her. Maybe she was right, and he should've broached the subject of him applying for a position in Sydney. But he'd wholeheartedly believed he was doing the right thing by her, and himself. After all, she'd been making plans for her agency without telling him, and that had been going on longer than his application for the Rose Bay GP's job.

Staring through to the lounge, his gaze alighted on Anna's painting. It was superb. Filled with passion. As though by finally following her dreams, her heart had spilled out on canvas for everyone to share. A heart that was devoted to Marty and their children—as well as herself.

That's what Vicki had intimated she wanted. To follow her dreams with him at her side. He hadn't disagreed. Neither had he said let's find the right place for the agency and he'd find a job wherever that was, because he was excited about his own possibilities in Rose Bay. It could be perfect for them both.

So could moving to Cairns.

The lights flickered. Stayed on.

He'd head home in the morning and give her some space so that hopefully everything would calm down and then they could talk again. They had to. It couldn't end like this.

CHAPTER TEN

HAD SHE REALLY said that? Vicki lay on her bed, staring up at the ceiling, ignoring the tears filling her eyes. It had sounded selfish even to her, but if she wasn't going to look out for herself, then who was?

Cole.

The pain in his eyes, tensing his body as he'd listened to her, had whacked back at her. She'd caused that. Hurt them both. There was so much he'd not told her until now. Yes, he would look out for her if she asked. He might even have heard how she felt over his choices. But apparently he'd found his dream job and she doubted she could ask him not to take it. That would be like Cole asking her to give up the idea of her agency.

She could run it from Rose Bay. From anywhere really. Was she being too harsh? Expecting everything to go her way from now on? But that wasn't what she was doing. She just wanted to have the life that suited both of them, where they could be happy again and she could stop worrying about being left on her own during the times she really needed support. She wanted to follow her dreams, and Cole's. It could be done. If he was open to her ideas. He had sounded okay with the agency. Had he thought how it might impact on him, especially if they had a family?

The light flickered.

Vicki held her breath.

The flickering stopped, the light remained on. She breathed.

They'd been lucky so far with the power still being on in Palm Beach. Damon had phoned earlier to warn her there were outages in other areas and it could happen here. Now that the rain was easing, perhaps there'd be no more.

Flicker.

Tempting fate, that was. Again she held her breath, again released it.

She was still in full, golden light.

Then she wasn't. Darkness filled the house abruptly. Black. Dense. Frightening. Sitting up, she waited for some natural light to filter through the windows so she could discern furniture shapes and the doorway.

'Vicki, you all right?' Cole called along the

hall. Then he was in the doorway, his shape darker against the low glow from a torch he held.

'Sort of.'

'I've turned the barbecue on to cook the remainder of the steak. Want to join me?' He was keeping himself in check, speaking as he would to anyone, not with the verve and love he usually had for her.

She could do the same, friendly but careful. 'I'll make a salad or butter some bread.' Standing up, she slipped her feet into the turquoise sandals by the bed. She wasn't going around in the dark with bare feet. Next she tugged a lightweight jersey over her head.

In the kitchen, Cole started quickly emptying the fridge of everything they might need for dinner so that they wouldn't open it again and lose what cold air was inside.

Vicki tried not to get more uptight. The power could be off for many hours with the electricity supplier already busy with other outages, and she going to have to get through the night without relying too much on Cole. That wouldn't be fair after what she'd said. Placing her torch on the bench, she reached for a lantern and struck a match to light it. After setting it on the table, she lit the second one. 'These'll make me feel cosier.'

'The rain's definitely lightened a lot. We

might see the end of this by the morning.' Cole carried the oil and steak out to the deck.

Vicki followed him, and looked out over the yard. She shivered. 'Mum and Dad are lucky. The lawn will dry out fast enough, and the house hasn't been affected.' Cole would know she was trying to fill the threatening silence. Awkward. 'I'll make a salad.'

Inside, she went about preparing a green salad, taking regular peeks at Cole as he stood by the barbecue, waiting to cook the steak. What *was* he thinking? He probably wanted to get out of here as soon as possible but she doubted he'd leave while there was no power to light up the place. Despite being cross with her, he wouldn't do that.

After shaking dressing over the salad she pushed the bowl to the side. Done. Now to butter some slices of bread. Basic but good food. Her favourite. And Cole's.

The silence grew as they ate, and Vicki couldn't relax. Her skin felt cold, her head pounded. She'd told Cole to go back to Sydney, but here he was, sitting opposite her having a meal. So normal and yet completely abnormal. Should she try to talk some more about his plans for joining the medical centre? But what more could she say without repeating herself?

'Relax, Vicki. I'll be out of your hair first thing in the morning.'

Her fingers tightened around her fork. Now that he'd put it into words she wasn't so sure she wanted him to go. But he had to find out if he'd got the position, and think about what he really wanted before they could talk about *them*. If they did. 'Your flight's in the afternoon, isn't it?'

'Yes, but I'll try to change it. If I can't then I'll fill in the hours in town.'

He hated wondering aimlessly around shops, could only stop for a coffee for a short time before he became restless. 'I'll drive you in.'

'We'll see.'

It wasn't as though he had a lot of choices. Taxis were most likely thin on the ground with the weather bomb playing havoc with the roads. Refraining from pointing that out, Vicki said instead, 'I'll boil some water on the barbecue for tea.'

'Let me do that.' He was up and finding a pot before she'd moved.

'Fine.' She'd rinse the plates, and try to find something else to keep her busy. It wouldn't be the ironing or watching TV. Picking up her phone, she checked for messages. 'At least we've still got phone coverage.'

'What about internet?'

'Not strong, but it's there.'

Molly had texted.

You all right?

No power but otherwise okay.

She'd call tomorrow and fill Molly in on the landslide and their role in helping the family.

What about Cole?

Molly wasn't letting her get away with just mentioning the storm. He's returning to Sydney tomorrow. Which was sad, but necessary if he was to figure how to go forward.

Tapping another text, she replied to her mother's query about how the storm had affected Palm Beach.

Saturated and no power, otherwise unaffected.

Joe from the medical centre had also sent a message.

You all right up there?

Yes. Been busy helping injured people, but we're fine, thanks.

Liar, liar. Not telling Joe her position with her husband.

'Gumboot or strawberry tea?' Cole asked.

'Gumboot, thanks.' Her gaze wandered to the glass door leading onto the deck, and the red and yellow floral painted gumboots standing just outside, and she smiled. She loved them. They beat the plain old black variety most people wore.

'Here.' Cole placed her mug on the table and went through the pantry until he found a packet of chocolate biscuits. He joined her and checked his phone. 'Nathan's texted.'

'Molly did, too.'

They were good friends. Nathan had always been, and Molly had fitted in perfectly. She'd turned Nathan's life around, had given him a second chance at happiness, as he had for her. He'd won her over by showing her not all men were abusive, didn't use their fists to prove a point. She was very happy for the pair of them. Across the table she saw Cole texting, his finger purposeful on the buttons, his mouth not as tight as it had been earlier. Hard not to lean over and wrap her hand around his. But she mustn't. He'd take it as an indication she was going to back off fighting for herself.

'Think I'll turn in. It's early, but what else is there to do?'

He paused his messaging and looked up at her, a sharp gleam in his eyes.

She had to ask that? In the past they'd have gone to bed all right, but there'd have been nothing to do with sleeping going on between the sheets. Hot memories roared into her mind and heat flowed up her cheeks. She spun away. 'See you in the morning before you go.'

Cole's heart was heavy as he watched Vicki sidle down the hall, a lantern in one hand, a torch in the other as she glanced left and right.

Sweetheart, it shouldn't be like this. We love each other.

The light on his phone faded, bringing him back to what he'd been doing before his heart had got side-tracked. He finished texting Nathan.

Internet's sporadic. Can you look up flights out of here early tomorrow for me?

He'd head home and drive around the Rose Bay area to get the feel of the place, try to look at it from Vicki's point of view. If she was determined to set up the agency it could be done from home, but she'd also want to take on some of the temp jobs that came in herself so a lot of travelling around the city would be an issue.

Though that would happen wherever they decided to live, and the bay was only a few kilometres from the city centre, which was a plus. They could make this work, he was certain of it, and then they'd get back to normal. Maybe try for a baby again.

'What else is there to do?'

Her question reverberated in his head. Make love again, slower than before, touch, kiss, explore. Yeah, that one explosive moment had only been the beginning to what usually followed on when they got together after time apart. That and lots of hugs and sleeping spoon style, and waking up at all hours for more kisses and sex.

Vicki had been thinking of that too. Her face had reddened immediately after she'd asked that question, and then she'd hastily departed for the bedroom. But she'd been too late. He'd recognised her response and known the same himself. Unfortunately, it wasn't happening. He would not push the barriers. He'd lost too much ground already. For Vicki the marriage seemed over. But not for him.

Nathan came back with flight details and, given the thumbs up, changed his booking. Sadness enveloped him. He did not want to leave Vicki like this, but she'd made it plain she wanted nothing more to do with him at the moment. It was better to focus on sorting out what he could in Sydney than hanging around, trying to get her to see reason. If he did get the job he could relax, knowing he had work he wanted, and then concentrate on helping Vicki with her plans for the agency and anything else she might want.

Scrolling through his contacts, he found the number he wanted and sent a brief text. As soon as a reply came back, he pocketed the phone and, armed with a torch, he headed to his bedroom.

The landline rang as he passed Vicki's room. 'Want me to get that?'

'Yes. Hope we're not needed again.'

She can't have been banking on that hope, though, because when he returned moments later Vicki was dressed and tying the laces of her navy shoes.

'A supposed heart attack.' He gave her the address before ducking into Marty's room to get the first aid gear and defib.

'We'll take the car. It's a little way along the main beach road.'

Silence landed between them as Vicki backed out onto the road.

He waited as she drove carefully through the deep puddles. Then, when he couldn't bear it any longer, 'What's up?' Which of their problems was putting that strained look on her face that he saw in the glow from the dash? Which was top of the list?

At first he didn't think she'd answer, then she surprised him. 'I worry I'm being selfish.'

That he had not expected. 'Why would you think that?'

'I'm not used to putting my foot down over what I want. Not on the big issues anyway.'

'Okay with demanding chocolate ice cream instead of vanilla, but not where to live?' Yes, that was his Vicki. Now the ball was in his court. Had he taken advantage of her indecisiveness?

'In a nutshell. But why? I've never been a wimp.'

'You like keeping everyone happy.' Why hadn't he seen that before?

'Now I'm including myself.'

'So it seems.' He didn't know where that left him; if she still wanted him in her life or not. She'd told him to go back to Sydney and sort out his own future. She hadn't included herself in that picture. 'It's okay. Better than okay. You have to be happy before you make other people happy.'

She said nothing.

Frustration got the better of him. 'I thought you were happy with me. That we were so in love nothing could come between us.' He clamped his mouth shut. Too much, Cole.

'I was,' she sighed. 'It all went wrong. Just go back to Sydney, Cole. Sort yourself out, and let me know what you're doing if you still want to.'

The sadness taking over her mood caught at him, turned his gut into a roiling pool of longing mixed with his own sadness. Thank goodness they pulled into a driveway just then. He could focus on a patient, let his head clear for a while. Forget the elephant between them. Forget? Sure. Try ignore it for a brief time. That was as good as it was going to get.

The front door swung open and someone flashed a torch in their direction. Grabbing the kit and defib from the back seat, Cole headed to the house, aware of Vicki right behind him.

'Dr Cole Halliday,' he said to the man standing before him looking desperate. 'And this is Vicki Halliday, a nurse.'

'It's my sister. She's having a heart attack. Lots of pain in her chest. I've called the ambulance.'

'That's good. Show us where your sister is. What's her name?' Cole nodded down the hall. *Hurry up. This is urgent.*

At last the guy moved. 'Sandra. She started complaining of pain an hour ago. In here…' He indicated a room where lanterns gave out an eerie light. 'That's my partner with her. Nadine.'

Why wait until now to get help? 'Hello, Sandra, Nadine. I'm Cole, a doctor, and this is Vicki, a nurse.'

'Hello, Vicki, how's things? Sorry to get you out in this weather.' Sandra was looking at his wife.

'No worries.' Vicki smiled at their patient as she reached to take the defibrillator from him. 'Had nothing better to do.'

Thanks a bundle.

'Where's this pain?' he asked.

Sandra tapped to the left of her sternum. 'Here. And here.' Her hand splayed across her upper abdomen.

'On a scale of one to ten, ten being the highest, how strong is it?'

'Five, though there are peaks when it's probably about eight.'

Vicki leaned over. 'You need to remove your top so I can attach the defib.'

Sandra gave her a wonky smile as she began lifting her tee shirt over her head. 'No problem.'

Cole studied the woman before him as he lifted her arm and felt for her pulse. Her colour was good, her eyes clear apart from the worry about her possible condition. Under his thumb her pulse was regular. Heart attack? Or indigestion?

Vicki had the pads on Sandra's chest and was

connecting the lines leading to the defib. 'How long has the pain been going on?'

'At least an hour, maybe more. I first felt uncomfortable after dinner.'

Glancing at the defib screen as it came to life, Cole nodded. 'Eat in a hurry, by any chance?'

Nadine piped up. 'We all did. Wanted to get it out of the way while we still had power.'

Vicki glanced up at him, a smile lifting her mouth, relief in her expression.

Again, he nodded. But he wasn't done that quickly. There were things to check and note down. The steady beats resonating in the stethoscope said normal heartbeat. Sandra's even breathing backed that up. The temperature Vicki showed him read thirty-seven. Checking the line on the defib screen once more, Cole relaxed and gave the news. 'There's nothing wrong with your heart. I'd say you've got a bad case of indigestion.'

Sandra stared at him, struggling to take it in. 'Really?' she squealed. 'Not a heart attack?'

'No. See how even those peaks are?' he tapped the screen. 'That's good.'

'Really good,' Vicki confirmed. 'Cole wouldn't have you on about something so serious.'

Sandra let out the breath she was holding. 'I'm sorry to be such a nuisance. Especially in this weather.'

'Do we cancel the ambulance?' Nadine asked.

'Normally, they come regardless once a call has been logged,' Vicki said, 'You are still having pain, Sandra.' She looked to him. 'What do you think?'

That I would like to go back a year—or more—and start over.

'That we need to err on the side of caution. It is normal to send someone in this situation to hospital regardless of the results.'

'There you go. Decision made,' Vicki said. 'I'll leave these pads on until the paramedics arrive.'

She was onto it. Better safe than sorry. Although Cole doubted Sandra had a medical problem, he'd have done exactly what Vicki indicated. If there was an area where they were always in sync it was when they were working with patients. Funny how they hadn't known that before this weekend.

'The ambulance's here.' Sandra's brother stood in the doorway, hopping from one foot to the other.

'That was quick for the circumstances,' Nadine said. 'I'll feel happier with you going to hospital, Sandra.'

'Me too. My chest still hurts, though not as much as before.'

The drive back to Marty and Anna's house

was quiet, though comfortable this time. The animosity had taken a hike, for a while at least. Shifting one way and another in his seat to ease the aching in his left leg and his back kept him busy for the few minutes before Vicki was pulling into the garage.

'Power's back on.' She stated the obvious.

'When did that happen? It was off at Nadine's.'

'Or they'd turned all the switches off and didn't realise the power was back.'

He supposed that was possible. Hoisting the pack over his shoulder, pain stabbed him. He gasped.

'You okay?'

'Fine.' Didn't have to tell her about every ache. 'Want a drink before hitting the sack?' he asked. It would be good to chill out together. They didn't have to talk about their relationship, could just be quiet, or chat about inconsequential stuff. If that was possible, given she'd told him to go.

'No, thanks.' She removed the defib from the back of the car before he had a chance.

Figured out he was hurting, had she? 'I'll take that,' he said stubbornly.

'I've got it.' Pressing the button to close the garage door, she headed inside and down the hall to put the gear away.

As she went into her bedroom, he said, 'I'll be gone by sun-up.' He got no reply.

He didn't know if that was better than a good-bye or not. Collecting his overnight bag from the bedroom he hadn't used, he headed to the kitchen where he grabbed a beer before settling into the large comfy recliner chair in the lounge to wait out the hours until his taxi arrived. No point trying to sleep when there were so many thoughts battling for supremacy in his mind.

Just when he'd thought he had his future organised he'd learned he had totally screwed up. Apparently, his own career didn't fit in with Vicki's idea of owning a business. Working in the Rose Bay centre was a golden opportunity to get established as a GP in a good area for raising kids. He'd believed he was doing the right thing by them both. How wrong could a bloke be?

Slugging down a mouthful of beer, he stared into the dark corners of the lounge. Apparently, he hadn't listened to her.

Well, sweetheart, you haven't exactly made yourself available for phone chats either.

Anger was rising amongst the confusion and hurt. There were two people in this marriage, in this mess. Both were responsible for decisions affecting each other and themselves. The guilt he'd felt at not being there for Vicki when the miscarriage had occurred had never gone away, not even when he'd refused to call her to come to him after the accident. That had been a mistake. The fear of being a paraplegic when he'd first come round and couldn't move his legs had made him desperate for Vicki to be with him. When he'd finally been reassured his spine was fine, he'd cried for her. Yeah, he'd been an idiot not to let the CO call her. Pride had done that to him.

But he *was* working at making amends in the only way he knew, and she was turning him down. One of them had got it all wrong. Worse, it might be him. Not a lot he could do except return to Sydney, go for the final interview and await the outcome of that before making any rash decisions that could backfire on him.

Vicki heard a car door slam and rolled onto her back, glad that the sun was finally lightening the room. Not wanting to bump into Cole and swap more anger and bitterness, she'd stayed in bed long after wanting to get up and do something, anything, to ease the tightness gripping her body. She hadn't had a wink of sleep and knew he hadn't used the bedroom next to hers so must've stayed in the lounge all night after they'd returned from Sandra's.

The house was too quiet as she made her way to the kitchen, where she reached for the kettle. Two empty beer bottles stood neatly on the bench. Where was Cole? Then she saw the pad on the table, and her heart slowed. He'd left without saying goodbye. Of course she'd told him to go. She'd meant it, and she hadn't. Well, she had if they couldn't find a way out of the hole they found themselves in. At least she could be proud for sticking up for what she wanted. Couldn't she? This was so crazy. Needing to look out for herself definitely came with consequences.

Her fingers were shaking when she picked up the note.

I got an early flight so ordered a taxi. Take care.
Cole XX

'Take care' as in have a good life? Was their marriage really over? Sinking onto a dining chair, she dropped her head into her hands and let the tears come. She'd got what she'd asked for. And hated it. She should've tried harder. One more honest, share-everything conversation surely could've saved their marriage? They'd talked about many things, shared a lot, yet still it hadn't been enough. Deep down she really hadn't wanted, or expected, them to come to this. He hadn't even let her take him to the airport when they might've been able to talk some more and come out the right side of their problems.

Now what?

She needed to get on with her plans for the nursing agency. Find a job to support herself in the interim. Where was the excitement she'd known when thinking about her own business? Gone in a cloud of longing for Cole. It seemed she couldn't have both.

Lifting her head, she stared around the dining room and then into the lounge. Her gaze landed on her mother's painting of Palm Beach in a storm. Her heart stalled. Since Mum had finally begun following her dreams she'd become like a flower in the sun, bright, pretty. Looking into the picture, Vicki felt the wind on her face, the rain on her skin, hear the waves breaking on the beach. How did someone do that with a paintbrush? Because Mum believed in herself, in her talent, her passion for art.

I have to believe I can have my dream. And hopefully my man.

CHAPTER ELEVEN

MONDAY MORNING COLE was up early, dressed in a navy suit and tie with a crisp white shirt, ready for the interview with hours to spare.

He wandered around the apartment, picking up photos Vicki had left behind. The two of them at their wedding, on their honeymoon, riding the waves at Bondi Beach—make that trying to ride them.

There was another taken the day he'd joined the army. He wore his officer's uniform and Vicki wore an enormous smile. Yes, they'd been okay back then. More than okay. They'd been so in love that even in the middle of a crowd there had been times they hadn't noticed anyone else.

I miss that so much I ache all the time.

Was it worth going to this appointment when, if he got the position, chances were Vicki wouldn't join him here in Sydney?

Jumping to conclusions here. He might not get the job. That wasn't a problem. He'd been on the net and seen other opportunities within the city and further out in the suburbs. Though Rose Bay did fit the bill of what he'd thought would be right for him and Vicki and their family when children came along. Right now, all he could do was wait and see how the interview unfolded. Only then could he talk to Vicki about making a commitment to living here. 'Together,' he added under his breath.

Putting the last photo back on the sideboard, he picked up his phone. No messages from Vicki. Not that he'd expected any, but a man was allowed to hope. Of course she wouldn't wish him luck if she didn't want to move back here. But then again, Vicki was usually fair, and always supported him in any endeavours he chose to undertake, so this was unlike her.

There hadn't been a peep out of her yesterday either. He'd respected her silence, and hadn't tried to get in touch. But he'd checked his phone numerous times until finally he'd left it in the bedroom so as not to pick it up every five minutes.

To hell with this hanging around.

He'd head to Rose Bay now. There were cafés there and by the time he'd made it to the township his stomach might be ready to take in some breakfast. If not, he'd go for a walk along the beach until it was nine o'clock, get a feel for the place he wanted to make home.

He did neither. His stomach wasn't playing ball, neither was the weather. Rain seemed to be the favourite pastime of the skies wherever he went at the moment. But at least this was a passing squall, not a monsoon. He actually smiled. Was this Vicki dumping on him to get his attention? Giving in to his need, he tugged his phone out of his pocket, and texted.

How's things up there?

She came straight back, making him wonder if she'd been waiting to hear from him.

Drying out slowly. You?

Getting rained on.

LOL

The phone went quiet. No good luck wishes. No questions about yesterday and what he might've got up to. Not a lot, but she might've asked. He hadn't even made it over here for a look around, had been too busy on the internet looking up other vacancies around the city—and in Cairns.

He went and found a coffee, to hell with his grizzly stomach.

* * *

Vicki set her phone aside and scanned the notes for her next patient. Cole would be on his way to his interview. She should've wished him luck. Not that he'd likely need it. He had a strong CV, and his time in the army might be a plus as he was used to different situations where patients were under trying conditions making them fearful and nervous. Maybe not what he'd see in Rose Bay often, but it gave him insight into people's mindsets he might not have gained otherwise.

'Vicki, Amelia Green's here,' the receptionist called through the door.

'Coming.' Quickly scanning the notes on the screen in front of her, Vicki focused on work and Amelia, putting Cole on hold. 'Hello, Amelia, come through.' She led the twenty-two-year-old through to her room. 'I see you're heading to Vietnam.'

'I can't wait. I've heard nothing but wonderful comments about the place.'

'So have I. Take a seat. So you're here for your Hep A and B shot? You know it's all in one now?'

'Yes. The doctor told me that when I first asked what I needed. He said to be aware of rabies and if I get a dog or monkey bite to go straight to the nearest hospital for an injection.

Or I could have the vaccination before I go, but I think I'll go with the first suggestion.' Amelia handed over her vaccination card. 'I had the typhoid shot when I went to Eastern Europe.'

'Right, I'll fetch the vaccine and we'll do this. Was it explained that we like you to wait for twenty minutes afterwards in case of an adverse reaction?'

Amelia nodded. 'I can finish an article on Iceland I started reading before you called me in.'

'That your next country to visit?' Vicki asked. She'd never had the travel bug the way Amelia seemed to. Too busy training and then being married to think about disappearing overseas. Europe and Britain had been fun, but hadn't lit a spark to be dashing off all over the world.

'I'm thinking about it. The Northern Lights look spectacular in photos.'

'Right, a sharp prick here.' Vicki inserted the needle, pressed the plunger, and it was done. She stuck a small plaster over the site. 'There you go.'

'Just like that. Thanks.' Amelia was gone, no doubt eager to get back to that article.

Vicki checked her phone. Lots of texts. Nothing from Cole. Eight forty-five. He wouldn't be at the medical centre yet. Was he nervous? Cole? He hadn't changed that much. Would he get in touch after the interview? She had to talk to him, to hear his voice, to know what was going on.

After filling in notes on Amelia's file, she clicked on the appointments screen. Next was thirty-three-year-old Mandy Stanaway, requiring external sutures removed post-mastectomy. Ouch. That was young. The patient file showed the results had come back and that Mandy had been referred for chemo and radiotherapy.

In the waiting room sat a woman in a wheelchair who looked Vicki's way the moment she entered. 'Mandy?'

'That's me.' She began wheeling towards her. 'I haven't met you before.'

Vicki put her hand out to shake. 'Vicki Halliday. I'm a temp nurse while Sarah's on maternity leave.'

Returning the handshake, Mandy smiled. 'Her daughter's gorgeous. I bumped into them in the supermarket yesterday.'

Crikey, the woman might look wan and worried but she wasn't sitting at home, fretting about her future.

I could learn something from her.

'Come on, let's get you sorted.'

It didn't take long to remove the stitches. 'All done.' Vicki pulled her gloves off while Mandy awkwardly pulled her top back on. 'Want a hand?'

'No, I'm fine. The stretching just gives me a nudge, that's all.'

'Any concerns about anything? You all right for pain meds?' One of the GP's would write a script if needed.

'Meds are good, got more than enough. And the stuff worrying me you can't help with. The chemo is the unknown factor: how I'll react to it and how long it'll take to get over the effects. Only time will tell.'

'I'm afraid you're right. Though we can arrange an appointment with a counsellor if you'd like.'

'The hospital offered the same, but I'd rather talk to family and friends first.'

'Fair enough, but know help is there if it gets too much. Is your partner supportive?' The notes said Mandy lived with a truck driver who was away a lot.

'He's brilliant.' Then Mandy's face fell. 'When he's at home. His work takes him all over Northern Australia for days at a time. We talk at least twice a day but sometimes it's not enough, you know?'

All too well. 'Will he be able to get time off when you're having treatment?'

Please tell me yes.

'The company's promised to juggle the roster as soon as I have a date to start chemo so that he can be with me for a few days around each treatment.' Mandy pulled herself up and fixed a smile on her face.

Like I would've for Cole, given half a chance.

Excellent coffee in hand, Cole sat with the three partners of the medical centre in the cramped office of one of the doctors, and waited for the opening gambit. It seemed odd having a third interview, which had him wondering if there was more to this.

'You picked the wrong weekend to visit Northern Queensland,' Jill said with a welcoming smile. 'We half expected to hear that you hadn't made it back.'

'The airport was open on and off Saturday, and all day yesterday. Vicki and I were kept busy helping the emergency services a lot of the time I was in Cairns.'

David asked, 'She's a nurse, isn't she?'

They knew that from a previous meeting, and from what he'd seen with these people they would not forget. Cole nodded, and waited.

'Where's Vicki working at the moment?'

'Temping at a family medical centre in Cairns.' What was this about?

Jill looked at the other two men and nodded.

Jason sat forward and clasped his hands under his chin. 'Here's the thing, Cole. We're impressed with your medical record, and more importantly we believe you'll fit in well with our patients.'

Unsure where this was going, Cole merely said, 'Thank you,' and sipped his coffee while he waited.

Jason continued. 'We have decided to bring in a fourth partner. We'd like to offer the opportunity to you. Obviously, the terms and conditions would be different and entail an initial financial cost to you, but the benefits would make that worthwhile.'

Just as well he'd swallowed the mouthful of coffee. Spluttering it across the desk would not look good. 'Thank you.' A partnership had been in his plans but he'd believed that would be well into the future. 'I'm interested.'

You never discuss things with me.

Vicki's accusation echoed around his skull. He hadn't said he'd take the partnership. There was a lot to find out about what was on offer before anything else. Couldn't deny his pulse was racing with excitement, though. Who'd have thought he'd get an offer like this so soon after quitting the army? When he hadn't experienced general practice work? It could be perfect. If Vicki went with the idea. 'You'd better fill me in on the details.' First things first.

* * *

An hour later Cole stepped out into brilliant sunshine and stood on the steps leading to the centre's parking area, taking deep breaths as the offer he'd just been made buzzed around his head. It was a very good proposal. He could afford to buy into the business, and the returns would be way beyond what he'd have earned if he signed on simply as a GP with the practice. The amount of leave available was more than he'd have expected for a partner, which could be beneficial if he and Vicki had children. The location fitted his idea of a good family suburb. He liked the partners, and the other staff he'd met at the end of the meeting. It had even been suggested Vicki could work there. What was there not to be thrilled about?

What would Vicki think? Would she jump on board, or say she wasn't prepared to move back to Sydney? One thing he was certain about. She wasn't about to forego her agency.

Anguish filled him. It was a hurdle to overcome. Admiration nudged at his anguish. She wasn't going along with his needs without fighting for her own. She'd not done that before, and it was probably gnawing away at her determination to keep focused. She needed his support, not his selfishness.

There was one way to find out. Staring at his

phone, he debated with himself. Ring her with the news? Or fly back up there to tell her face to face? Gauge her reactions and try to answer any negatives she came up with? He wasn't accepting the position without talking to her first. He *had* learned that much.

Striding out along the steaming street, he headed for the town centre, looking around at the homes he passed, then the stores where people stopped and chatted to each other. A good sign of a friendly neighbourhood.

With a takeout coffee and a salad roll in hand, he headed for the beach to sit on a damp bench and enjoy the view of Sydney Harbour. Ferries plied between many of the bays and downtown Sydney, churning up the water as they zipped back and forth. Above, seagulls squawked as they swooped for any scraps lying around. Adults walked their dogs on the beach. Picture perfect. And he'd had a very tempting offer to become a part of the scene. To establish himself as a GP in a lovely neighbourhood was something he'd been dreaming about for a while.

Yet now it so close to happening, he felt uncomfortable. As though something wasn't right. Something was missing. Vicki. Yes, absolutely. But there something else itching at his excitement and he didn't know what it was. Tossing the paper cup and paper bag into a rubbish bin,

Cole strolled along the beach, nodding to those who said hello, patting dogs that came to sniff him. It was easy to feel he might belong here. But…

Vicki.

The woman he loved, had sworn to love for the rest of their lives. The woman he'd fallen for the moment he'd set eyes upon her. She'd been there for him every time he'd returned from an overseas posting, had listened as he'd poured out his grief and anguish about the sights he'd witnessed, the desolate people he'd tried to help. Basically, she'd backed him all the way, all the time, until she couldn't take it any more. And look how he'd repaid her. Badly.

The warm sun on his back loosened some of the tightness in his muscles, but it didn't help the sense he was making a mistake. There was something else going on here. If only it would stand up and let him identify what it was.

Go to Camperdown.

With no idea why that had popped into his head, Cole turned around and headed back to town and the car, sensing that a visit where his time in Sydney had begun might help solve his dilemma.

The old stone brick building of the medical school Cole had trained at loomed large when he strolled up to the front. Memories of the first time he'd ever walked through the main entrance filled his head. He'd been nervous, excited, and glad to be starting there. He was starting afresh. In a large city where most people remained anonymous, where he could hide in plain daylight, and not be approached regularly to be asked how he was getting on now his name had been cleared, or told it was so sad what had happened and how he had to let it go and forgive every one for thinking he could ever commit such a crime.

Cole jammed his hands in his pockets and stood staring around, his legs splayed, his head spinning, and his heart beating slowly as he absorbed the familiar surroundings.

I chose this medical school because of its location in a large city where I was a stranger.

It helped that it was one of the best in the country, too, but that had come second to the need to just be a medical student learning his trade. It had worked. He'd made friends, met Nathan who had eventually became his closest mate. And he'd finally put everything on the line by telling Nathan what had gone down back in Adelaide when he'd been a teen. Nathan, being the guy he was, had clapped him on the back and dragged him down to the pub for a beer. No criticism, no unctuous comments about how he was sure Cole wouldn't have stolen the money, just a bloke's way of saying *You're fine, mate.*

It had felt good and it had been the last time he'd felt the need to explain himself to anyone as a test of friendship.

Sorry, Vicki. I made a mistake there.

Driving along the streets towards the run-down house he'd shared with four other students, he stared around. So familiar, so different. He wouldn't like to live here again. He was a doctor now, didn't need the shambolic lifestyle of a student. Neither did he need to hide any more. Now he could walk down any street anywhere, head held high.

Cole pulled to the side of the street and pulled on the handbrake, leaving the motor idling. He was getting closer to whatever had begun to irk him as he'd walked on the beach. It took time to make friends in a neighbourhood where everyone was intent on their families and careers and getting ahead. Especially in a huge city. Not like Cairns. Bet if he bumped into Merv or one of the other rescue crew members he'd worked alongside during the weekend, they'd stop and chat, probably suggest a beer at the pub or to go round for a barbecue. They'd certainly acknowledge him.

Am I ready for that?

More than ready, he realised. He wanted it,

for himself and Vicki. For their children. To be comfortable, relaxed, and happy. The army hadn't given him that picture. It hadn't been bad, just not what he'd been looking for. It hadn't included Vicki, for one. And there wasn't anyone more important to him.

No one.

'Jack, the crutch is not a bat,' Vicki admonished as her patient flicked a large stone down the medical centre's drive.

'Not a very good one, anyway.' Jack laughed. 'I couldn't get the dog's bowl up the steps this morning.' He'd been in to get his dressings changed.

Rolling her eyes, she grinned. 'You're hopeless.'

'I hear you and your man were busy Friday night, rescuing that family from their ruined house. Everyone's been singing your praises at the station.'

'We did no more than the fire crew did. It was a joint effort, with good results.'

We. As in her and Cole. *We.*

A sigh slid across her lips, and her mood dipped. Again. Still not a word from him. She'd given up checking her phone for messages last night, tried to accept he wasn't rushing to tell her how the interview had gone. Except every time the phone pinged her heart would leap and she snatch it up only to be disappointed. Everyone but Cole seemed to be in touch. This morning she'd left the phone in her bag and refused to take it out all day. There could be a message from Cole by now, for all she knew, but she wasn't looking until she walked out of here in half an hour's time to go home.

Did his silence indicate she'd got what she'd asked for? What if she was wrong to demand he sort himself out before they went any further? What if he never called her again?

Jack was still talking. 'So the guys are wondering if you'd be interested.'

'In what?'

Now it was Jack's turn to do the eye-roll thing. 'Sorry if I'm boring you.' His smile told her he wasn't cross. 'Would you like to join our station as a voluntary medic?'

Become a part of the fire crews? Sounded exciting. Bit like working in an emergency department without all the modern equipment and a whole hospital to back the medics. It would fill in some more hours. 'Yes, I think I would.'

'Right, let Damon know. We're having a meeting on Wednesday. I'll put a word in for you.'

Guilt reared. 'Um…slow down. I would like to help, but I'm not sure how long I'm here for. I might be returning to Sydney soon.'

Might. Probably won't, because Cole has given up on me.

'Come on board anyway. We'll put you through the training, and if you leave town your time, and ours, won't have been wasted. We need people like you, Vicki. We really do.'

Pride swelled in her chest. 'Thanks. Okay, count me in for as long as I'm here.'

'Need a doctor as well?'

Vicki spun around, lost her balance, would've fallen if Cole hadn't caught her.

'Steady, sweetheart.' He gazed down at her with an intensity that tightened every muscle in her body.

'You didn't call me once.'

'Thought it better to come in person. Far more intimate.' He leaned closer, brushed his lips over hers.

She had to fight not to press back, to devour him with a kiss. Every cell ached with the need to touch him, feel his tenderness, to believe he really was here, holding her. 'Cole?'

'Yes, Vicki, I'm here, hopefully for good.' His gaze remained on her. 'If you'll have me.'

'Yes.' Just like that? Well, she wasn't carrying on feeling lonely and sad when this was the one person who made her happy. And he was here. 'With some changes,' she added through a smile.

Cole's return smile filled her with gladness. They would make this work.

'I can see I'm in the way here,' Jack interrupted them. 'I'll get in touch tomorrow. And, yes, we can always use a doctor. Now, where's Barbara got to?'

'She went next door to the pharmacy,' Vicki told him, and instinctively headed out to help him get into the car, feeling a loss as Cole's hands slid away from her arms.

Cole followed. 'I'm Cole Halliday, Vicki's husband,' he told Jack.

Jack grunted with pain as he lifted his cast leg inside the car. 'Jack Henderson. I've heard about you. Talk later when you've got a spare moment.' He grinned at her, then nodded to Cole. 'Go on. Seems you've got things to sort out.'

'You stay off those quad bikes, and bend down to pick up the dog bowl. There's nothing wrong with your waist.' She closed the door on Jack and turned to face the love of her life. Had she given in too quickly? When she shouldn't be giving in at all?

'Relax. I'm not here to demand we do everything my way. What time do you finish for the day?'

Joe was walking up the drive with a pharmacy pack in his hand. 'You can go now, Vicki. I'll cover for you if anyone needs a plaster put on a cut. Good to see you, Cole.'

'There's no one else booked in for me,' she said in a wobbly voice. 'So thanks, I'll grab my bag and get out of here.' She didn't look at Cole, just headed inside as quickly as possible, her head spinning at his sudden appearance. She'd said yes, she'd have him back, without thinking it through. She'd acted on her love for him. It was right. Now she still had to make sure he understood she wasn't backing down from her plans.

When she returned Joe and Cole were talking.

Joe held out his hand to shake Cole's 'Talk again.'

'Sure.'

'What was that about?' Vicki asked as they walked to her car.

'Work.'

'Right.' Back to not telling her what was going on? A timely reminder they hadn't resolved everything. But…she breathed out hard… Cole was here, with her, and he wanted to fix what was keeping them apart.

Clasping her hand, he said, 'It's okay, I promise. I just want to start at the beginning.'

'Then jump in and I'll drive as fast as I can because I need to hear this.'

'How about we find a quiet corner in a bar along the waterfront instead?'

'Sounds like a plan.' She knew exactly where to take them. As long as she wasn't getting her hopes up too high. Sneaking a sideways glance, she saw that Cole appeared relaxed yet edgy at the same time, giving no clues about what had gone down in Sydney so she hung onto his words back at the medical centre and tried to relax. Yeah, right.

Cole sat beside Vicki at a table on the pavement and looked at her. There were deep shadows staining her cheeks, and her mouth drooped. Equally, her eyes gleamed with what he could only recognise as love.

'I've been offered a partnership at the Rose Bay Medical Centre.'

She flinched, then rallied. 'You must be thrilled. That's great news.' Locking her eyes with his, she said, 'I mean it, Cole. I'm proud of you. Not that I'm surprised. You're a great doctor with the people skills required to make patients trust you.'

'I haven't accepted. I'm probably not going to.'

Her eyes widened.

'I haven't said anything to the partners yet. I wanted to talk to you first. To decide together where to live.' This was about their future, not just his.

'Tell me more.' Could those beautiful blue eyes get any wider?

'The contract has everything I want, yet it doesn't sit right with me.' Sipping his wine, he reached for Vicki's free hand, entwined their fingers. She didn't jerk away. 'That's wrong. It was Sydney I needed to look at properly. I went there as a teen to get lost in the crowds, to be free of people approaching me to talk about the theft I didn't commit. Being in a large city worked. I got on with study and making friends who knew nothing of my past.'

'Then I don't see what the problem is for you to continue living there.'

'I'm not saying I've made up my mind not to. But the other night, helping the rescue crew, I felt right at home with everyone without having to prove anything to myself or them. It's as simple as that.' Turning to face her, he locked his gaze with hers. 'I want to live where we'll both be happy. Have a job that fits round your dreams too. I love you, Vicki, and that's all that matters. Everything else can be worked around, but not my love for you.'

She studied him with an intensity he was coming to know. There was no anger or sadness, only hope in that expression. 'I never stopped loving you, Cole. I needed to be heard, that's all.'

'And hugged when everything was going belly up.'

She nodded. 'That too.' A devastating smile broke out on her face, and knocked his heart sideways.

Leaning closer, he wound his arms around his woman and covered her mouth with his, and kissed her long and deep, like he'd never kissed her before.

Pressing against him, her breasts on his chest, Vicki returned the kiss with equal vigour and love. The longer they kissed, the more his body softened—though some areas tightened. The months of tension evaporated, to be replaced with the love he hadn't stopped holding for this beautiful woman.

The sound of a metal chair leg scraping on concrete cut through the wonder 'I love you,' he whispered as he lifted his head to look around.

Beside their table an old man was getting to his feet. 'Good luck, you two.'

Vicki laughed. 'Thank you, but I don't think we'll need it now.'

Cole grinned. They were back on track. He waved to the waitress. 'Could we have two glasses of your best champagne, please?'

'Coming right up.' The young woman was smiling. 'Very quickly.'

Vicki pushed her barely touched glass of wine aside. 'That'll have to take a back seat if I'm having bubbles. I'm driving, remember?'

He slid it across to her hand. 'We're not going back to Palm Beach today. We're going to spend the night here in town at that hotel you can see.' They'd be together, make love, eat in bed, drink some more champagne in the hotel where there wouldn't be any interruptions from Vicki's family or friends. 'Ironic when I said I didn't need to remain isolated any more and here I am, wanting a night totally to ourselves.'

'Here you go, you two.' Champagne flutes appeared before them. 'Enjoy.'

'Oh, we will,' Vicki lifted a glass and wound her arm through his. 'To us.'

They sipped.

'That's nectar.' She smiled.

'It is.' Hang on. He still had something to say. 'Vicki, wherever we choose to live, I will help with your project, give support in any way you require. When we have a baby I'll do my share of parenting so you don't have to juggle everything too much.'

'We can do all of this in Sydney, if you would like to take up the partnership. I have no beef against Sydney. It's a great place to live—together.'

'We'll talk about it. Later.' He tapped their glasses together. 'To us,' he repeated her words. 'I love you.'

'I love you too.' Then she burst into tears.

EPILOGUE

Twelve months later...

VICKI STEPPED OUT of the car and smoothed the skirt of her cream full-length dress over her six-month baby bump and down to her new cream suede, solid-heeled shoes. The heels, thicker than normal, were to keep her upright in the sand. Anyway, they looked awesome.

'Are we ready?' Damon looked directly at her, a cheeky grin on his face.

She laughed. Did that a lot lately. Then she looked around at the group standing with her on the walkway leading down to the white sands of Palm Beach. 'What do you think?' she asked her brother. She was as excited as the first time she'd done this. More so, really, now that she and Cole had resolved their differences and were living together all the time, sharing their lives as she'd always hoped for.

'Then let's do this.' He took her arm as Phil stepped up to take the other.

'Can't have you falling flat on your face.' Phil grinned.

'I wouldn't be flat with junior in there, making a hill out of my stomach.'

Behind them, her father said, 'Anna, Julie, let me escort you both down to the beach. I've been made redundant with Vicki by my sons.'

Everyone laughed. It had been decided days ago that her brothers were walking her along to Cole where he waited on the beach with his father, and Nathan and Molly with the twins, to renew their vows. Cheeky guys that they were, Phil and Damon reckoned they might bring a bit more luck to the equation this time.

'Let's go.' She laughed. 'Can't keep Cole waiting.'

'Why change now?' Damon quipped.

'Because today, and only today, he can have everything his way.' Tomorrow they were going on a second honeymoon, back to Rarotonga and the same luxurious resort.

'Bet he'll be too busy making sure you have everything you want to be thinking of himself,' Julie said from behind her.

Yes, Cole put her first so often now it could get embarrassing. Despite being busy with the medical clinic he'd bought into here in Cairns, he'd backed her all the way with the agency, which was already doing well. Not so busy there weren't days when she had no jobs to fill, but those were becoming fewer and fewer.

Stepping onto the sand, Vicki looked along the beach to the small group waiting for them all. Her heart lurched with all the love spilling out. How could she once have thought they were over? It wasn't possible. She loved that man waiting for her more than life itself. And now they were going to be parents, were expecting a tiny miracle to love and cherish for ever.

She stumbled. Love was so wonderful.

'Hey, clumsy, look where you're going.' Phil grinned.

'There's a big distraction just ahead.' She grinned back.

'You two…' Damon rolled his eyes '…need to find a hotel quick smart.'

'Not until after the ceremony,' she retorted. Then she was standing in front of Cole, her heart flapping around in her chest like a fish on sand, and nothing else, no one else, mattered. Reaching for his hand, she held on tight, never wanting to let him go again. 'I love you,' she whispered.

Cole leaned close to brush his lips across hers. 'And I you.'

'Hey, you two. Enough of that. There are decent people present,' Damon's laughter broke through the haze taking over her head. 'And the marriage celebrant.'

'You saying I'm not decent?' Karen asked with a twinkle in her eye.

They didn't legally require a marriage celebrant to renew their vows, but she and Cole had become friends with Karen and Arlo since the monsoon, and when Karen had heard about the ceremony there had been no stopping her partaking in it. Not that either of them had wanted to turn down her offer.

'Right, let's do this.' Karen shuffled the pages in her hands as she waited.

Vicki and Cole turned to face her, still holding hands.

Here we go, second time lucky, Vicki thought. *Luckier.*

Karen started with something unexpected. 'I am so glad you picked a beautiful, sunny day for this celebration, nothing like the night we met under a hill.' When everyone chuckled, she added, 'That was the worst time of my life and yet Arlo and I now have two wonderful friends we didn't have before.' She glanced across to her husband with a tender smile just for him.

Arlo winked. 'Get on with it, woman. The champagne's getting warm.' His foot tapped the Esky at his side.

'Cole and Vicki, do you both vow to love and

cherish each other for the rest of your lives? To support and care for one another? To raise your family surrounded by love and understanding? To share the good, the bad, and everything in between with love and have a smile for each other every morning?'

Vicki's breasts rose as she drew in sun-warmed air and gazed at the man who was her husband, her support, her soul mate, her love. 'Yes, absolutely. I'll always love you, Cole. Always have, always will.' Her throat clogged up with unshed tears. She wasn't going to cry today. This was a joyous occasion.

Cole's hands were shaking as he held hers. 'Vicki, my heart. I promise to do all those things and more. I love you with everything I have. And some,' he added as a tear slid slowly down his cheek.

She rose on her toes to wipe the tear away with her finger, then leaned up to kiss him. Another tear appeared on his cheek. Okay, maybe crying was allowed.

'Not so fast,' Karen interrupted.

Laughter bubbled up from Vicki's tummy. 'Like Arlo said—hurry up.'

'Cole and Vicki, man and wife, we all wish you both the very best for the future and in everything you do. Your love is strong and beautiful. Enjoy.' Karen stepped back. 'Cole, you may kiss your wife.'

'About time.' His arms wound around her and she was hauled close to his strong body that had continued to strengthen back to normal over the past year.

Vicki knew nothing but Cole. His lips on hers, his man scent, his love pouring into her. This was her man, her life, her everything. They'd done it. Overcome the odds and found a stronger happiness together where each felt comfortable to talk about anything that worried them, which was surprisingly little these days.

Then someone tapped her on the shoulder. 'I'm so happy for you.' Molly. There was a river streaming down her face.

Turning in Cole's arms, she reached for her friend and hugged her tight. 'Thank you for everything.' The support, the understanding, and the celebration when she and Cole had learned they were having a baby.

'How is baby? Any reaction to her parents' special day?'

Looking down at her swollen belly, she had to laugh. 'Last time I swapped vows with Cole I could see my shoes. Not a chance today.'

Cole swung her up into his arms, lifting her legs so she could see her feet. 'There you go. Looking glam, if I might say so.'

'Not bad for a pair of swollen feet and toes like little sausages.' Then she leaned in against his chest and returned to kissing him. To heck with the champagne. Kisses were far more exciting. And important. 'Here's to us.'

'To us.'

And his mouth claimed hers, giving her a taste of their future. All good and exciting and filled with love.

* * * * *

If you enjoyed this story, check out these other great reads from Sue MacKay

A Fling to Steal Her Heart
The Nurse's Twin Surprise
Taking a Chance on the Single Dad
Redeeming Her Brooding Surgeon

All available now!